STRAIGHT BACK

A NOVEL

BY DAVID MENON

David was born in Derby, England in 1961 and has lived all over the UK but now he lives in Paris, France. In 2009 he gave up a long career in the airline industry to concentrate on his writing ambitions. He's now published several books including the series of crime novels featuring Detective Superintendent Jeff Barton that are set in Manchester, UK and the series of Stephanie Marshall mysteries set in Sydney, Australia. He's also created the DCI Sara Hoyland series beginning with Fall from Grace. Apart from being a full-time writer he goes off two or three times a year to teach English to Russian students for a school in St. Petersburg. His other interests include travelling, politics, international current affairs, all the arts of literature, film, TV, theatre and music and he's a devoted fan of American singer/songwriter Stevie Nicks who he calls the voice of his interior world. He loves Indian food, a gin and tonic that's heavy on the g and light on the t, plus a glass or three of red wine. Well, it doesn't make him a bad person.

www.davidmenon.com

www.facebook.com/davidmenoncrimefictionauthor

www.amazon.co.uk

Short story collections

- Kind of Woman.

- Losing Grip.

This is for Gill … and for Karl and Sandra.

ONE

The Shadow Home Secretary Martha Langton was in the Victoria, London flat she shared during the week with her husband, fellow politician and Labour party front bencher, Nick Langton. They were having a flaming row. It was all to do with the document that had been passed anonymously under her office door at Portcullis House where many MPs have their Westminster offices and which was joined to the House of Commons by a tunnel underneath the road that divided them.

'Look, you've dealt with it, Martha' Nick pleaded. He was standing in the doorway between the kitchen and the living room. He was still in his suit trousers but he'd taken his tie off and undone the top couple of his shirt buttons. He'd also rolled up his sleeves. He'd cooked dinner because he was the better cook and he was now seeing to the pots. He had a tea towel slung over his shoulder and with his dark hair he didn't look unlike one of those Italian restaurant owners who does all his own cooking.

'Not all of it, I haven't' said Martha, looking up from the Evening Standard that she was reading at the table.

'Martha, there's a whole paedophile ring been discovered because of what you passed on to the police' said Nick, with his hands on his hips. 'I don't need to tell you that the scandal has been seismic and it's already made you a hero'.

'Yes I know and I'm not interested in being a hero, Nick' she countered. 'I just did what any responsible citizen, let alone politician, would do, to bring individuals to justice for heinous crimes that they've got away with for too long because they're well connected with the establishment. Christ, one of the reasons I'm in the Labour party is to bring an end to the establishment being able to cover its own bloody arse'.

At least twelve arrests had been made of prominent members of the entertainment industry, the legal profession, police officers and politicians who'd been involved in a paedophile ring in London during the seventies and eighties. The arrests had all been made because of information contained in the anonymous document that had been passed to Martha. It had left the governing coalition with a lot of egg on its face and the Conservative Home secretary Angela Carter had given Martha the kind of praise at the Commons dispatch box that must've made her run for the sick bucket as soon as she was out of the House. Angela hadn't asked Martha during their private briefings why she thought the document had been passed to her rather than Angela herself, but Martha was sure she'd be itching to know. So would Martha for that matter and the only conclusion she could draw so far was that Martha, being a Labour politician who hadn't gone to public school and whose family wasn't part of the acknowledged establishment, had been sufficiently detached from all the people accused in the document of wrongdoing that she wouldn't be sufficiently compromised by any relationships with any of them. On the other hand, Angela Carter, it turned out later in the more detailed press coverage, had family connections with several of the names contained therein.

'I still can't quite get over the extent of it' said Nick. 'Although I suppose it shouldn't surprise me. There have been such strong rumours for years'.

'Which we sat on when we were last in office, Nick. We're no better than anybody else here'.

'But this is where it stops, Martha'.

'Nick, the paedophile ring isn't the only crime that document reveals'.

'I'm aware of that, Martha but as I said before that's where it stops'.

'Nick, you cannot be serious'.

'Martha, we've been through all this'.

'I know'

'And I thought we'd sorted it'.

'No' said Martha as she folded the paper up. 'You decided that I wasn't going to do anything with the other information. I had no part in that decision'.

'Oh here we go again'.

'Meaning?'

'Meaning this is going to be one of those times when you accuse me of reverting to being the alpha male domineering his little woman'.

'And I'd be right'

'No, you wouldn't' Nick insisted. 'Martha, we've always taken all our decisions together. And we've always given each other the veto. We both have to agree or it doesn't happen'.

'This is too big and too serious, Nick'.

Nick stood for a moment and breathed in deep. His wife was right that this was too big and too serious and it was for that very reason that he believed they should stay silent. The consequences if Martha revealed what they knew from the rest of the document could not be measured hypothetically. But they were enough to make Nick think they should leave well alone.

'The reaction to the discovery of the paedophile ring will seem like nothing compared to what would happen if the rest of it breaks' said Nick. 'And I'm thinking of the safety of our family'.

'And you're saying I'm not?'

'I'm saying that you can kiss goodbye to becoming party leader after the election if you go public with this'.

'That's if we lose the election' Martha corrected. She knew that Nick and the current party leader were at absolute loggerheads on almost everything and there were rumours that the leader was preparing to drop Nick from the Labour front bench and not see him journey from shadow cabinet to governing cabinet if Labour wins. Martha's knives for the leader weren't quite as sharp as Nick's although she wasn't exactly the leader's biggest supporter within the shadow cabinet. This was where her emotions were often conflicted but it was inevitable when both you and your husband were senior politicians. 'But if I don't do something with this information, if I just sit on it and let the guilty go unpunished then I can kiss goodbye to my conscience'.

'Yes, well I'm not sure if having one is a positive thing if you want to be party leader'.

'Stop twisting it, Nick'.

'I'm not, darling, I'm just … Martha, you know the consequences if you reveal the rest of what's in that document. I'm asking you to think about the family, Martha. I'm asking you to put them first'.

'Are you saying I don't do that as a matter of course anyway?'

'You know that's not what I meant'.

'So what did you mean then?'

'I mean that as much as I know you and as much as I love you, I also know that you'll end up doing what you think is best. And I have no say in that'.

TWO

Sheridan Taylor hated her life. It hadn't always been the case. She used to love it. She used to think she must be one of the luckiest girls in the world. She used to have a horse. That was now gone. She used to have friends from families who were equally as well off as her family was. Now she'd be too embarrassed to pass them in the street. She used to have a Mum, a Dad, a sister, and a big Alsatian dog called Brutus. She adored Brutus. He was the family dog but he was her dog. She could always get him to do whatever she wanted. None of the others were able to do that. When they'd had to leave their house they'd had to give him away to the police because the housing association who owned the property they were moving to didn't allow pets. He was out there somewhere catching criminals now. It had broken her heart the day they took him away. She'd cried for days afterwards. She'd never forget the look on his face as he stared helplessly out of the back window of the van they drove him away in. He was barking like mad. He didn't want to leave her. She didn't want him to leave.

She walked through from the kitchen and in the living room her Gran was minding the new baby for Sheridan's Mum.

'He's a beautiful little thing' said Joan who couldn't take her eyes off her new grandchild Tariq.

'No, he isn't, Gran' said Sheridan who wasn't going to let herself get swept up by all the emotion over a stupid brown baby. 'All babies are ugly'.

'Look at that mass of black hair and those dark eyes' Joan gushed, ignoring Sheridan's bad-tempered dismissals.

'Yeah well, that's what you get when you've got a darkie for a father' snarled Sheridan.

'Sheridan, that's enough' Joan warned who was running out of patience with the way her eldest granddaughter had been behaving lately. 'You're being rude and offensive'.

'Well don't ask me to care because I couldn't care less'.

'Don't you speak to me like that young lady'.

'Well, I'm not in the mood for a lecture either, Gran so save your breath'.

Joan stood up and raised her finger to Sheridan. 'Your mother has been too soft on you, Sheridan for far too long. I know you've been through a hard time but so has everyone else in the family and you're no different'.

'Gran, you've gone as soft as everyone around here. Am I the only one who can see that Arif doesn't belong in this family, in this house or even in this country?'

'And why do you think all that, Sheridan?'

'Because he isn't white and English like us and he's given me a half breed brown brother that I absolutely refuse to love'.

'He's also a good man who mended you mother's broken heart'.

'Oh here we go again' said Sheridan. 'You're going to start bad mouthing my Dad'.

Joan saw red and had to stop herself from smacking Sheridan's face. 'Well yes it might help to go over some of the things your precious Dad did to destroy this family. He took your Mum out to one of the swankiest restaurants in Manchester only to tell her that he'd lost all their money and once the meal was paid for that was it. He left you all the very next morning to go and run a health spa in the south of Spain with the woman he'd been having an affair with behind your mother's back. Do you ever hear from him? No. Does he ever ring you or email you? No. And that's all because he basically doesn't give a damn about you'

'That's not true'.

'Were you listening just then? You're deluding yourself, Sheridan. Your Dad was a total failure as both a husband and a parent'.

'You're a liar!'

Joan recoiled in shock at the ferociousness of Sheridan's verbal attack. 'I've already asked you to watch what you say to me, Sheridan'.

'My Dad wouldn't have just abandoned me and our Paige like you're all making out he did! You just want to make him out to be a really bad person and you're all liars'

Joan broke her heart when she saw her granddaughter cry. Sheridan had been a real Daddy's girl. She'd idolized her father, Joan's ex son-in-law Brian, and could never believe anything bad about him despite the obvious truths. She wished he could see the damage and the heartbreak he'd left behind.

'Sheridan, if your Dad is seen as a bad person then he's done it all by himself'.

'And why are you happy for your daughter to be with a dirty Arab?'

'Sheridan, where did you get your prejudice from? Neither your Mum, nor your Dad for that matter, brought you up that way. Arif is taking good care of your Mum and he wants to take care of you too if you'd let him'.

'I don't want to even look at him'.

'A bit difficult that when you're living in the same house'.

'I wish he'd just go away and leave us alone'.

'If you only knew what Arif had to run from in Iraq … '

' … well tough, okay? He can run right back there for all I care. There's too many like him in our country and we need to send them all back'.

Joan kept having to remind herself that her granddaughter was only fifteen years old. She spoke like she had all the emotional baggage and resentments of someone much older. She was so unlike her sister Paige who was only two years younger but had an older and more mature head on her shoulders. When their father Brian had declared himself bankrupt and gone off to Spain leaving the family with no money, Joan's daughter Ellie had been forced to uproot her two daughters from their home and from their lives and move them into temporary accommodation provided by a housing trust in the Ancoats area of Manchester. It had been two years since then and they were still there. The neighbourhood wasn't brilliant and it wasn't what they were used to but there were some good people around and Ellie had managed to make some good friends and so had Sheridan's sister Paige. But Sheridan had remained obstinately opposed to doing anything positive to at least try and settle down.

'Mum drove Dad away' said Sheridan between sobs.

Joan was beside herself with frustration. 'That's not true, Sheridan'.

'It is true'

'But it isn't true, Sheridan. One day you'll have to accept that he deliberately hid money away that belonged to his family, meaning you, and used it to start his new life in Spain'.

'You mean I've got to listen to lies from you and Mum. Well I won't do that, Gran. I will not do it!'

'Sheridan, I really don't know what to say to you any more'.

'Well you don't have to say anything because I will never accept a darkie as my step-father and I'll never accept that half caste bastard as my brother!'

Joan couldn't stop herself this time and slapped her one. 'Now I'm sorry but you deserved that, Sheridan. Tariq is your flesh and blood! He'll be looking to you his big sister to help take care of him and there's so much for you to be proud of if you'll only open your heart and let both Arif and Tariq in. I'm scared Sheridan because I just don't know you anymore. What happened to the little girl who used to come and stay the weekend with me and bring her colouring books and I'd plait her hair? That little girl would never have been so horrible to a defenceless little baby, especially when he was her little brother. If your Granddad could see the way you're acting now it would break his heart'.

'Finished?'

'What?'

'Because I've had enough and I'm going out' said Sheridan as she made for the door.

'Where are you going?'

'As far away from this joke of a family as I can get'.

'Sheridan, stay and let's talk' Joan pleaded. 'Sheridan!'

'I don't want to therefore I won't'.

Sheridan left her grandmother reeling and stormed out of the house. It had all been so easy at the old house with the old life that had been so cruelly ripped from her. All anybody goes on about now is how happy her Mum is with her brown boyfriend Arif and how happy they all were for her. But were they mad? Didn't any of them see what Sheridan saw? The stupid foreign bastard came out with words in English that Sheridan had never even heard before. What was his problem? Why did he have to talk like English was a language that Sheridan didn't understand? She'd always been dead set against her Mum going to work at that refugee centre. She'd told her she'd be mixing with all the dregs from the rest of the world who'd thrown themselves at Britain because we were such a bloody soft touch but she wouldn't listen. She'd said she'd wanted to help people. What the fuck did that mean? She should've started with her own family.

There was a large expanse of waste ground behind where she lived and Sheridan loved to wander across it to be alone with her thoughts and right away from everybody. She felt safer with all that open space around her than she did in the tightly knit streets of where she now had to say that she lived. She knew that some of the other kids in the neighbourhood hated her but she couldn't care less. They could all go to hell. They were all losers who'd do nothing with their lives except have babies with dead loss idiot men. Well they were welcome to it. Sheridan was determined never to have kids and as soon as she could save up enough money she was going to Spain to be with her Dad whether her Mum liked it or not.

She didn't know then that she was being followed.

She looked up ahead as she fell into parallel steps with the elevated electrified train lines heading for Manchester Piccadilly station a couple of miles away. She was going to get on one of those trains one day. She was going to get a one way ticket and never come back to this dump. She could see the big Hilton hotel that towered over everything else in the city centre. She could see one of the other big posh hotels in the city that was right next to the station. Posh people with loads of money stayed in places like that. She knew that because once upon a time her own family had been amongst them. That was before Dad lost the business but it can't have been all his fault. She'd never accept that.

She got to the main road and on the other side was a petrol station with a kind of mini supermarket attached to it. She had some money and she thought she'd get some crisps and chocolate that she could eat in her room later so she wouldn't have to join the rest of them at the table for tea. How can you have a proper conversation with someone who doesn't speak your language properly and when there's a half caste bastard baby who grabs everybody's attention and keeps crying all the time? She hated the way her sister Paige had accepted the whole situation and the way she liked to play mini-Mum to the brown bastard Tariq. What the hell was she thinking? Didn't she want their Dad to come back? How could he come back now that brown bastard was here? How could life ever get back to normal again?

The road was a dual carriageway and she managed to get across by running and then jumping over the central reservation. She walked across the forecourt and into the shop. She chose two large bags of crisps, three chocolate bars, and a pot noodle just in case she got really hungry. When she took them to the counter her arms sort of collapsed and all her stuff scattered across the small space. The man behind the counter lifted up a carrier bag and began to put her things in it. Sheridan didn't like this at all.

'Oi, that's my stuff!'

'Yes, and I'm helping you by putting it in a bag'

'Sorry?' she questioned. The man was another darkie just like Arif. Why don't they all go back to where the fuck they came from?

'Didn't you hear what I said to you?'

'I heard but you're not speaking proper English so I couldn't understand'.

The shop assistant took a deep breath. 'I said that I was helping you by putting your things away in a bag. That's all'.

'And you see I still can't understand because you're not speaking English!'

Sam Jackson was standing behind Sheridan waiting to pay for the petrol he'd just filled his car up with. This girl in front of him was being so bloody rude to the guy behind the counter and Sam hated that. He had to intervene.

'Look, love' said Sam. 'I understood this gentlemen perfectly well. He was trying to help you and you're being rude'.

Sheridan was incensed. 'What the fuck has it got to do with you?'

'Don't use language like that to me'.

'I'll do what I fucking well like!'

'Oh come back and talk to me when you've grown up'.

'I beg your pardon?'

If there was one thing Sam couldn't stand it was teenagers like this girl talking to adults as if she'd just stepped in them. He especially didn't like the racist overtones in her abhorrent behaviour and despite the fact that the guy behind the counter was gesturing for him to say no more and that it was okay, it wasn't okay as far as Sam was concerned and he'd continue to stand up for the guy.

'But you can start now by apologizing to the gentleman'.

'No way! Why are you standing up for him? You're a white person. He's just a stupid Paki who shouldn't be here'.

'How is somebody as young as you so full of hate?'

'How is somebody like you not sticking up for your own race?'

'You're out of control. Somebody should sort you out'.

'Really? Well somebody should stab you'.

'That's your answer to everything is it?'

'No. But it's my answer to you'.

Sheridan always carried a knife with her whenever she went out. It was for protection. But this time she was going to use it to teach this stupid bastard that he should stick up for his own race of white people. She took the knife out of the inside pocket of her jacket and lunged it at Sam whose attention had been taken by a conversation with the guy behind the counter. He didn't even see the knife coming until it was too late and it penetrated his skin just below his heart. He immediately went into shock. The guy behind the counter pressed the alarm button under the counter and then came running round to try and help Sam. He looked angrily at Sheridan and said 'The police are coming you stupid, horrible girl'.

'You made me do it!' Sheridan screamed. 'It was your stupid fault!'

She went running out onto the petrol station forecourt and that's when she first saw the car as it came screeching round from the back. She stopped dead in her tracks as the car moved out in front of her and the window on the driver's side rolled down.

'Sheridan, get in!'

Sheridan squinted her eyes in the late afternoon sunshine. Could it really be him? 'Where the fuck did you spring from?'

'Never mind that just get in!'

Sheridan looked down at all the blood on her clothes and started to cry. 'I think I've killed somebody'.

'Sheridan, I know, I saw it all happen. Now we've got to get you out of here before the police arrive so for God's sake get in! Trust me, I can get you out of this but we've got to leave now before it's too late'.

Sheridan ran round and jumped into the car on the passenger side. He then sped off down the main road towards the city centre. 'There' he said. 'Immediate danger over. I was watching you as you came across the wasteland. I wanted to protect you and step in if you got into any trouble. Good job I did, eh?'

'Did I really kill him?' she cried hysterically. 'Oh God I can't go to prison, I can't, I can't!'

He placed his hand on her knee. 'It won't come to that. Okay? Now you've got to trust me and everything will be alright. I promise you'.

'Where are we going?'

'To somewhere I can take care of you until all this is over'.

THREE

'Can you remind me how we got here?' Rebecca Stockton asked.

'Well we walked, or rather ran up the stairs once the mood had struck us' answered Joe Alexander.

Rebecca laughed. 'No, you silly bugger I know how we got up here and into your bed but how did we, you know, get here?'

'You came round for lunch but something else came up'.

Rebecca laughed again. 'Am I going to get anything serious out of you this afternoon?'

'The way I'm feeling now I'd say the answer is a definite no'.

DI Rebecca Stockton and DC Joe Alexander had been in very different emotional places when Joe joined DSI Jeff Barton's team just a few weeks ago. Rebecca had thought she might be getting somewhere in her pursuit of Jeff Barton as a romantic as well as a working partner but her amorous intentions were thwarted once more by Jeff's admission that he still couldn't see past the death of his late wife Lillie Mae. Joe was getting over being dumped by his ex girlfriend whilst he was in hospital fighting for his life after an incident involving guns whilst on duty. Joe had taken the rejection hard. He'd never been that lucky in love and his adult life was sparsely populated by girlfriends.

Then one night at the pub last week something had happened. It was a kiss. A drunken kiss but a kiss that was no less intended than if they'd been sober. They'd both felt that shiver when you suddenly really notice someone rather than just noticing that they were there. It had got all of them talking at the station which neither of them wanted but accepted it would be the case. Rebecca was relieved however that Jeff Barton hadn't been there that night because he was still on his holidays in Hong Kong. She had finally accepted that there was no future for her and Jeff but she didn't want to appear to rub his nose in it or stick two fingers up at him by moving so swiftly onto the next man, especially when he was on the same work team which could lead to complications.

Nothing had happened that night of the 'kiss'. They'd got into their cars and driven away in their respective directions. The next morning they didn't go anywhere it. They didn't speak about it at all. There were lots of embarrassed silences and they both ran away from it all, not confronting it and not acknowledging it in any way.

Until earlier this morning when they bumped into each other doing their Sunday morning weekly shop at a branch of Tesco's that neither of them knew the other shopped at. For a moment they'd looked at each other and wondered what on earth to say. They were standing by the cheese counter. A quick look at their respective trolleys gave the game away. They were carrying the essentials like bread, milk, a chicken to roast, packs of vegetables to microwave, bags of bananas and apples, a steak, a couple of lamb cutlets, a couple of frozen pizzas. And half a dozen bottles of wine. They were both advertising the fact that they were single and having to fend for themselves with no surprise additional mouths to feed but they weren't planning to survive on junk food alone.

'What did you do yesterday?' asked Rebecca.

'Saturday? I slept in, I caught up on the week's papers, I wished it was Sunday and a day closer to going back to work. And you?'

'Pretty much the same' said Rebecca. 'Managed to avoid going round to see my friend who is not only head over heels with her new man but also pregnant by him'.

'You can only take so much of other people's happiness when you've no life of your own'.

'That is so true' said Rebecca. 'I'm happy for my friend. I'm happy for anyone who's happy. I just wish some of it would come my way for a change'.

'Yep. I know'.

'I hate weekends when we haven't got a case on' said Rebecca. 'I go to my parents and have Sunday dinner with them plus my sister and her family. It all goes fine until afterwards when my parents are sitting at the table with my sister and her husband and I'm in another room playing with the children as if I'm not worthy of sitting at the grown ups table because I'm not married and don't have children. Don't get me wrong, I love my nephews dearly and get so much joy out of being with them. But my life is stuck. It won't move on. And I'm in danger of staying this way and watching my nephews one day overtaking me and starting to go out on dates'.

'One of my nephews has overtaken me and is dating his first girlfriend' said Joe.

'You see? It happens'.

Joe laughed. 'And what sad bastards we are that we envy our nephews for their love lives?'

Rebecca decided it was time to take control. One of them had to do it and may as well be her. It was okay for women to do this sort of thing now. At least it was for some women. Rebecca had once got into a furious argument with a fellow woman police officer at a training day who was a strident feminist and felt that women hadn't spent years fighting for their equality only to use it to make themselves what she called 'easy' for men who are just wanting to score. She also hinted that it was unprofessional for a woman police officer to behave that way. Rebecca had countered by saying that her colleague was basically arguing for things to go back to when men who engage in casual sex use it to enhance their reputation whilst women who engage in it had their reputations destroyed by it. Well Rebecca wasn't going to stand for any of that nonsense. If she wanted a man who clearly wanted her but was too shy to say so perhaps because she was his senior officer then she just had to go for it.

'Joe, do you fancy going off to your place or mine and having sex? It could be the best alternative we can find to the whole family Sunday dinner thing?'

'I thought you'd never ask'.

Rebecca hadn't taken much notice of Joe when he first joined Jeff Barton's team along with DS Adrian Bradshaw. Of the two Adrian was the better looking and he kept himself in shape. But he was a widower and Rebecca had been through all that with Jeff. Trying to tell a widower how you feel, trying to work out how he feels about you, trying to work out when they'd decided it was time for them to move on and contemplate being ready for another relationship and then trying to work out if they were just using you to get back in the saddle. It was all a nightmare of heart shattering proportions. She was steering clear of widowers from now on. It just never ends well when you can't match up with a ghost.

But in the carnal sense she'd been pleasantly surprised by Joe. Adrian Bradshaw was better looking but Joe wasn't exactly ugly and she didn't have to force herself to enjoy being in bed with him. She hadn't drunk him handsome. And she was surprised at his stamina and sensitivity. Very pleasantly surprised.

'So what happens now, DS Alexander?'

'I go downstairs and bring us some wine up?'

'Yes that will work' said Rebecca as she stroked his shoulder with her fingertip.

'Have you enjoyed yourself?'

'So far so good'.

'You mean you expect me to do all that again?'

'Well I'm not going anywhere soon'.

'So demanding' said Joe who couldn't believe his luck. He'd woken up expecting another same old Sunday and ended up having wonderful sex with his senior officer.

'Get used to it'.

'You mean we're going to do this again?'

'Well, I don't see why not. Do you?'

They embraced and kissed and Joe was getting hard again. They began to position their bodies in order to seek further pleasure from each other when Rebecca's mobile began to ring.

'I'd better get that' said Rebecca.

Joe groaned and reluctantly pulled himself off her. Rebecca pressed 'answer' on her phone and Joe watched her expression change from one of flushed and unbridled pleasure to one of business and the job they both did.

'I'll be right there' said Rebecca who was acting up as head of the team whilst Jeff Barton was on holidays. She slid out from under Joe's duvet and began gathering her clothes together. 'Your further intentions are going to have to wait, young man. We've got a spot of murder to deal with'.

The pathologist June Hawkins had begun her work on the murder site and her team were diligently going about their business in the way that scientific types like them do.

'The act of killing is fairly straight forward here, darlings' said June who was in her full cover up suit all the way down to including her footwear. 'He was stabbed'.

'No kidding' said Joe. He'd accompanied Rebecca to the scene. There were always two of them at meetings like this and neither he nor Rebecca saw any reason to set it up as some kind of disguise. It was procedure.

'How are you Joe darling?' June enquired. 'I haven't seen you for ages'.

'I'm good, June, thanks' Joe replied with a sideways glance at Rebecca. Could it really be that they'd come straight from his bed to this crime scene? Well yes, that's exactly what they'd done. He felt like a naughty schoolboy who'd been caught by the headmistress watching porn even though June didn't know about that day's coupling. They had to stay discreet. It would be impossible otherwise.

'There was only one stab wound but it was close enough to the poor bugger's heart to kill him fairly quickly' June went on. 'She must've either been lucky or she knew just where to go with her knife'.

'So it was a girl who did this?' Rebecca questioned.

'Oh yes' said June. 'They're getting worse than the boys. Speak to your WPC. She'll tell you'.

WPC Josie Fletcher came up to Rebecca and Joe and after introductions had been made she explained what she knew so far.

'The shop's CCTV has captured the whole thing, ma'am' said Josie. 'Sunil Kumar was on duty here behind the counter. He said the man had been sticking up for him after the girl had been abusive towards him and that's when the girl pulled out the knife. They'd been arguing but the attack looked like it was unprovoked. Sunil says he recognizes the girl as having been into the shop before but doesn't know her name'.

'How old was this girl?' Joe questioned.

'I'd say she was no more than about fourteen or fifteen, sir. Apparently she went running out of here and was picked up by a car which then sped off. But there was no CCTV outside because the machine had broken and was waiting to be fixed'.

Rebecca rolled her eyes up. 'Typical' she said. She was desperate to get a grip on the case. She wanted to show the hierarchy that they'd been justified in placing her in charge of the team whilst Jeff Barton was on holiday. 'Do we have identification of our victim?'

'Sam Jackson, ma'am' said Josie. 'Thirty-six years old. It looks like he just stopped to get some petrol and this happened to him'.

'Where does he live?'

'In a flat in Salford Trinity, ma'am' said WPC Fletcher. 'In his wallet were a number of his business cards. It looks like he worked as a rep selling farm equipment'.

'Employer?'

'They're being informed now, ma'am. I'm also making further enquiries about his background'.

'Okay' said Rebecca. 'Thank you, WPC Fletcher that was very thorough considering you can't have been on the scene long'.

'Thank you, ma'am'.

'Not like you to praise uniform so enthusiastically' said Joe after Fletcher had stepped away.

'Well let's just say I'm in a good mood' Rebecca replied. 'Can't imagine why. Any ideas?'

'Must've been the Sunday lunch you had'.

'Yes well the portions were very satisfying'.

Joe blushed. 'I'm glad to hear it'.

'Right' said Rebecca bringing herself back to focus on the job. 'Let's look at that CCTV'.

After they'd watched the footage Rebecca ordered stills showing the face of the young girl attacker which she planned to release to the press. 'We'll need to get DS Ollie Wright and DC Adrian Bradshaw up to speed but before we do let's talk to our friend Sunil. He's sitting outside looking bloody terrified. Poor bugger'.

'He's no doubt afraid of what his boss might say about all this too' said Joe. 'You know how caring some employers can be. And he might be wondering if the girl might come back and target him. If not the girl then whoever drove her away. Right now she's clearly getting support from someone'.

'Exactly' said Rebecca. 'And the question is who and why?'

FOUR

'Okay then people so let's see what we have here' said DI Rebecca Stockton as she opened her first briefing in charge of the team. She hadn't bargained on her mouth suddenly going dry but used the opportunity to hand over to DS Oliver 'Ollie' Wright.

Ollie stepped up and addressed the squad. 'Our victim is Samuel Arthur Jackson' he said as he pointed at the photograph of the victim on the white board. 'Thirty-six years old. Divorced. His ex wife lives in Hazel Grove and he was on his way back from her house to his flat in Salford Trinity when he stopped to fill up with petrol'.

'That was one unlucky decision' said DC Adrian Bradshaw.

'It certainly was' Ollie concurred. 'Jackson and his ex-wife Karen shared custody of their two children, Ben aged nine and Hannah, aged seven. Karen is distraught at the news and hasn't yet told the children'.

'That's the toughest call a parent has to make with regard to their children' said Adrian who was taken back for a moment to when he had to tell his three children that their mother had been murdered. He still shivered when he thought about it especially in the knowledge that he was partly responsible for her being where she was at the time she was killed. If he hadn't been having an affair at the time then his late wife wouldn't have gone in pursuit of answers after being told malicious gossip. That brought her into the path of a killer. 'And I know'.

'You so do, mate' said Joe Alexander in support of his friend. Joe had been an invaluable friend to Adrian during the early days of Adrian's bereavement and they remained close although Adrian hadn't told Joe all the circumstances surrounding his late wife's murder.

Ollie let a moment or two pass before continuing. 'She says she'll keep them away from all that and then keep them off school tomorrow so she can tell them then. She and Jackson apparently parted on good terms, no animosity, just the realization that they weren't making each other happy anymore and they remained friends since the divorce. They had shared custody of the children'.

'But that they could all be so civilised' said Rebecca who wanted to strangle the girl who put out the flame of a seemingly good man who was still devoted to his family even after it had broken apart. They were a rare breed in her experience.

'Amen to that, ma'am' said Ollie. 'Now this seems to have been a random attack. It's not known if there was any connection between the teenager and Sam Jackson but judging by the nature of their exchange on the CCTV it wouldn't seem like they'd met before. What we need to know is who was driving the car that the girl escaped in and with such apparent ease?'

'They must've been known to her?' Joe reasoned. 'Why else would she just get into the car?'

'But how did they know to be there?' said Adrian. 'Were they following the girl?'

'That would be my bet' said Ollie. 'But for what reason?'

'And what were they going to do if the girl hadn't turned herself into a killer?' said Adrian.

'That's what scares me' said Joe. 'Whoever it was wouldn't have been following a teenage girl just to kill some time of a Sunday afternoon. I think they had other intentions. They might have been planning to attack her or assault her in some way'.

'So why would he continue in his pursuit of her once the crime had been committed?' said Ollie. 'Assuming it is a male we're looking for. Why wouldn't what happened scare him off?'

'He might've believed that he had even more of a leeway with her if he could make himself out to be the only one who could help her' said Adrian.

'You're painting what appears to be an increasingly likely scenario to me, gentlemen' said Rebecca. 'Do we know what the make of the car was, Ollie?'

'Yes ma'am' Ollie answered. 'It was a blue Ford Mondeo but we don't know the registration'.

'Okay' said Rebecca. She paused whilst she gathered her thoughts together and then looked at the three expectant faces in front of her. 'Well someone out there will know that the girl is missing. So I'm not going to the media with this until tomorrow morning'.

'With all due respect, ma'am, is that wise?' said Ollie.

'She may be a killer, ma'am', but she's still only a teenager who's probably scared out of her wits in the hands of some stranger and struggling to come to terms with what she's done?'

'I know what you're saying' said Rebecca. 'But look, I know it means taking a risk but if that picture we have of her goes live on the media somebody out there may be inclined to protect her and therefore not come forward with an identification. But if that same someone is worried simply because she hasn't come home for a few hours then they may contact us and lead us to that identification. And if nothing does come through tonight then I'll call a press conference for first thing in the morning and make sure a media blitz is carried out. I'd prefer it if I had your agreement, gentlemen? Ollie?'

'With reservations but yes, ma'am, I support you'.

'Thanks Ollie. Adrian?'

'The same as DI Wright, ma'am' said Adrian.

'Okay, thanks Adrian. And Joe?'

'With you, ma'am'.

'Right' said Rebecca. 'Now let's not forget that this girl may be vulnerable but nevertheless she's also a killer. I also want to start house to house around the petrol station. Somebody must've seen that Mondeo hanging about and I also want to appeal for anyone who passed the petrol station or was a customer themselves there at around about the same time as the incident occurred, to come forward and tell us whatever they know. I mean, it wasn't even dark. Somebody must've seen something'.

Shortly after the briefing Rebecca was called in to see Superintendent Geraldine Chambers who asked her how the investigation was getting started. Rebecca explained everything to her.

'So you're letting potentially valuable hours pass before going to the media' Chambers contemplated. 'Like to take such risks, do you?'

'I do have my reason, ma'am, which I've explained'.

'Yes, and I heard' said Chambers. 'And police work does require a certain amount of calculated risk taking. But you do realise I can't give you any extra resources, Rebecca'.

'Ma'am?'

'I can't give you extra personnel, extra officers to help you with this investigation. Our resources are stretched to the limit as it is so you'll have to do the best you can with what you've got. You're lucky. DSI Barton has built up a highly accomplished team and I know you can work with tight resources'.

'With respect I know that, ma'am. I'm part of it'.

Chambers paused before answering. Try as she might she'd never been able to warm to Rebecca Stockton. She'd wanted to. She'd wanted to support a fellow female officer as much as she could because God knows they still do need an extra push of encouragement. But Stockton was just one of those people that she just couldn't connect with.

'I know you have a complex personal relationship with DSI Barton'.

'Which never comes in the way of our work and never will' Rebecca replied in very measured tones. If the stuck up bitch was going to have a go at her about Jeff then she'd whack it straight back at her pinched up stupid face.

'I know that too' said Chambers.

Rebecca wondered why it was that she got the biggest grief within the police force from other women officers. It was like they wanted her to shine and yet they didn't want her to shine because that would reinforce their perspective against what they saw as the still male dominated world of police work. Rebecca had always been a bit of a tomboy. She preferred the company of men. That's why being the only woman on Jeff Barton's team didn't matter a jot to her. She could hold her own with guys without any problem whatsoever but what the attitude that Chambers was implying was that women officers like Rebecca were always victims of one sort or another, emotionally or professionally. Well Rebecca had never seen and could never see herself as being a victim. She'd focused and been a diligent police officer who'd earned her promotion in the same way that any comparable male officer had. She had nothing against any of the male officers she worked with. But attitudes like the one she was getting from Chambers irritated her beyond belief because they were supposed to be on the same side and by that she meant police officers on the side of the law.

'Ma'am, can I ask why, so early into this investigation in fact before we've really started, it was decided that we wouldn't get any extra resources? This is a murder investigation and the killer is a teenage girl who's gone missing in the company of someone who looked like they may have been following her'.

'Why do you ask the question, DI Stockton?'

'Because it doesn't seem fair that DCI Warburton's team who are investigating the stealing of champion horses from farms across Cheshire have been told that money and resources are no object'.

'Are you saying that one crime should be higher up some kind of pecking order, DI Stockton?'

'I'm saying that I've got a missing, potentially vulnerable teenage girl out there who's murdered a complete stranger and when the press work out, as they will, that we're prioritizing our resources around missing horses instead of missing teenagers, I can almost guess the headlines and the onslaught of criticism we'll get'.

'A potentially vulnerable teenage girl who you're not going to start looking for until the morning? Don't throw stones at your own glass house, DI Stockton. And if I were you, I'd concentrate my efforts on being the good police officer that you are. Don't use this opportunity of DSI Barton's absence on holiday to somehow play the maverick hero because I can assure you it doesn't go down too well with some who may be influential in your future career aspirations. That's all for now'.

Joe took Rebecca down for a drink at Salut Wines in the centre of Manchester just off Market street.

'When did you find this place?' Rebecca asked as they sat down at a table. 'I mean it's in the little more refined posh part of the city centre so I'm wondering how you found it?'

'Oh very funny excuse me while I laugh for a nano second' said Joe.

'And it seems quite sophisticated too' Rebecca added. 'The bar, the crowd, everything. Even you look sophisticated in here, Joe'.

'You're a cheeky monkey'.

'That's probably what Chambers thinks about me too' said Rebecca who was still seething from her encounter with the Chief Superintendent. 'God, I've let her get under my skin'.

'You have and you can't let her do that' said Joe. 'You're in charge. She hasn't said anything about you not being in charge. Therefore her support for your decisions is implicit in that'.

'Why am I acting like the bog standard neurotic female struggling to survive in a man's world? I sound pathetic. I sound like I don't deserve to be where I am'.

'Hey, hey, hey' said Joe, taking her hand. 'You do deserve to be where you are and you don't need me to tell you'.

'Joe, you are the most feminist man I've ever met who didn't lick the other side of the stamp' said Rebecca as she squeezed his hand tightly.

'I'll take this as a compliment'

'You should do' said Rebecca. 'And I know I've just got to hold my nerve'.

'You have' said Joe. 'It goes with the job. But you'll only maintain everyone's respect if you hold your nerve and stay true to your decisions, no matter how it works out. If you do that then nobody can reproach you including Chief Superintendent Chambers'.

Joe and Rebecca ordered a plate of meat tapas each along with a bottle of Bordeaux. Rebecca was having problems with feeling as relaxed as she did when there was such an intense looking investigation kicking off but as Joe said she'd taken the decision not to put things out to the media until the morning so perhaps it was okay to take a little time out whilst they could.

'So look, Joe, are you sure you're happy with our little arrangement?'

'Friends with benefits?'

'Yeah' said Rebecca. She pulled her hair back behind her ears with her fingertips. 'I use your body, you use mine, we have a laugh and there's no strings'.

'It's all very modern and grown up' said Joe who wasn't altogether sure if he did want this kind of casual fling at all. Maybe he was more keen on Rebecca than he'd ever admit to. But then again being a man with certain needs did mean that their arrangement put the smile back on his face. So who wants to get serious? Whenever he'd got serious with a girl before it had always ended in disaster and he really didn't need anymore of all that.

'It is' Rebecca agreed. 'Very Sex and the City'.

'So in that case are you going to start calling me Big?'

'Well that would make me Sarah Jessica Parker, right?'

'Right' said Joe. 'It would'.

The two of them were laughing when Rebecca's phone rang and during the conversation Joe watched her expression plunge from being happy and relaxed to being grey and troubled.

'What's up?' asked Joe after she'd finished.

'Get your coat, Joe' said Rebecca who picked up her jacket and handbag. 'There's a Ford Mondeo on fire as we speak behind a warehouse on Cheetham Hill Road. They can't see at this point if there's anybody inside'.

FIVE

'Did you have a look to see what's on TV tonight, Mum?' Leo asked as he loaded the dishwasher after he and his mother had finished dinner. He was thirty-two years old and it had always been just him and his Mum. She'd never told him anything about his father and he'd never asked. He just assumed that it can't have been a very pleasant situation when she got pregnant with him. Maybe his father had been married and left his Mum high and dry like so many others do. Maybe it was all just too painful for her to talk about. Either way he felt like she'd brought him up well even if at times he'd felt a huge sense of loss because it isn't true to say that you don't miss what you never had.

'I didn't yet, son, no' Catherine replied. She hadn't been home from work that long before she'd started on dinner. Her job at the records office of the Hope hospital in Salford was constantly under review which meant it was constantly under an implied threat. So far she was holding on but if they did decided to pay her a handsome sum with which to ride comfortably into retirement, she wouldn't object. In fact, she'd snap their bloody hands off. 'Aren't you going out tonight?'

'No' said Leo. 'I've quit drinking during the week just to give my body a bit of a break. I've said I'll see them all on Friday'.

'You don't mind if I continue to indulge?'

'Of course not' said Leo who'd finished loading the dishwasher and was now doing his best to enjoy sipping from a mug of tea. This no drinking business was so bloody boring. He could just go a nice pint now. 'Did you make that appointment with the doctor?'

'What can he say that I don't know already?'

'I didn't think you had' said Leo who was concerned that his mother's usual stubbornness might lead to a late diagnosis of something potentially serious. 'I want you to get everything checked out, Mum. You've not been yourself lately'.

'And what is myself, son?'

'You see there you go' said Leo. 'I've never heard you talk like this before'.

'Oh why did I have a son who's like a dog with a bloody bone'.

'Well you did' said Leo. 'And I know my Mum. And I know when she's in denial'.

Catherine knew Leo was right. The sharp, stabbing pain in her lower back had been growing in intensity and was starting to have a debilitating effect on her daily movements. She was fighting it because she was only fifty-eight and didn't want to start acting like an invalid. But she was scared to find out what it might be. She worked in a hospital. She was surrounded by sick people every day and like most medical staff she had no desire to become a patient.

'I'll ring the doctor in the morning' said Catherine.

'Do you promise?'

'Yes, I promise'.

'Good. Now go and get yourself settled down in the living room and I'll bring you a glass of wine through'.

Catherine smiled at the considerate nature of her son. He'd make some girl a very lucky wife one day but although he had a good social life he never seemed to meet anyone special. He'd had a few skirmishes over the years but he'd never got engaged or even really serious with anyone. He wasn't ugly or overweight. He wore decent clothes. He just didn't connect with the big game of life and love. It made her worry sometimes about how lonely he might get when she'd gone. It didn't seem to worry him though.

She went through to the living room and switched on the TV. With the remote control she pressed for Sky News. There was a time when she wouldn't have been seen dead watching or reading anything owned by Rupert Murdoch but maybe it was something to do with the landscape out here in Littleborough. From her living room window she could see right across the moors and it tended to mellow people. That and the fact she would also have to concede that she thought Sky was a pretty good news station. Sometimes better even than the BBC.

It was the second item that the presenter read out that caught Catherine's attention. Her mouth literally dropped open with shock. The item was about a missing teenage girl from Manchester called Sheridan Taylor whose body had been found in the wreckage of a burned out car. She turned her head to see Leo standing there with her glass of wine in his hand looking like someone had stepped on his grave.

'Wasn't she one of your students?' asked Catherine.

Leo swallowed. 'Yes' he said before giving her the glass of wine. 'I bloody need one of those too now'. He went back to the kitchen and poured himself a glass. He could feel his heart begin to beat faster and he leaned his forehead against the wall cupboard. He thought for a moment and then he nonchalantly looked up towards the front door and wondered how long it would be before the police came wanting to talk to him.

'I'd just like to say how very sorry we are for your loss, Mrs. Taylor' said DI Rebecca Stockton. She was sitting on a chair in the living room of the Taylor home with DI Ollie

Wright sitting beside her in the other chair. Ellie Taylor and her partner Arif were sitting opposite them on the sofa. Rebecca hadn't exactly expected a warm welcome but it looked like this encounter was going to be harder than she thought.

'Well I'm gratified I'm sure' said Ellie, her voice shaking with emotion. She was overwhelmed with grief but she was also bloody angry at the way the police had handled the case so far. 'I was wondering when you'd show up'.

'We came as soon as we thought it was appropriate, Mrs. Taylor' said Rebecca.

'As soon as you thought it was appropriate? You've got a bloody nerve. How come you didn't think it was appropriate to instigate a search for my daughter once you knew what had happened at the petrol station? How come you didn't distribute the picture from the CCTV before this morning when, as we all know now, it was too bloody late!'

Rebecca glanced sideways at Ollie.

'Oh don't bother looking at him' Ellie commanded. 'You are the senior officer in charge of this case, aren't you?'

Rebecca swallowed. 'Yes, I am, Mrs. Taylor'.

'Then I'm asking you to explain how my baby girl came to die all alone in a car that was on fire when you should've been out there looking for her?'

Rebecca was at the tail end of an absolute hell of a day. Not only had she received sideways looks of disapproval from other officers outside her team but the press conference she'd had to endure earlier had been like a lynch mob. They all wanted to know why the search hadn't been instigated once they had the CCTV picture and literally grilled Rebecca on it. But that all paled into insignificance compared to having to look the mother of Sheridan Taylor in the eye like she was doing right now.

'Mrs. Taylor, if I may' said Ollie by way of rescuing Rebecca. 'We had no way of knowing if it could've made a scrap of difference to release the picture of Sheridan as soon as we had it'.

'So why didn't you?' Ellie wanted to know. The fear of what her little girl might've suffered during those few hours was beginning to overwhelm her again, just like it had been doing all day since they'd found out. 'I mean, do you have any idea what might've happened to her during those hours she was missing and how the thought of that is killing me?'

'Do you know who the driver of the car might've been, Mrs. Taylor?' asked Rebecca.

'What?'

'Well it's clear to us that Sheridan must've known who it was otherwise she wouldn't have got into the car so easily'.

'My daughter may be sixteen but she's still at school and wouldn't know anyone who drives around in a big car picking up teenage girls' said Ellie.

'Then how do you explain why she went off in that car, Mrs. Taylor?'

'Oh I know what you're doing' Ellie snarled. 'You're trying to shift the focus away from your mistakes and onto the painting of my daughter as some kind of delinquent'.

'Mrs. Taylor, we're doing nothing of the sort, we're simply trying to work out what happened'.

'I'll tell you what happened. You didn't put her picture out quick enough which lost you valuable time. My daughter's death is on your hands, detective'.

Rebecca decided to take that one on the chin and keep going. 'Mrs. Taylor, the driver of the car is still out there and we're determined to find him so we can give you the kind of answers that may bring you some kind of peace'.

'Some kind of peace? Are you mad? I'll never find some kind of peace over this!'

'Okay, I apologise for the choice of words, Mrs. Taylor but we're doing everything we can with regard to this case'.

'You're a liar'.

'I beg your pardon?'

'You said at your press conference this morning that you'd put out a notice last night to all police stations in Greater Manchester telling them to inform you if there were any reports of missing teenage girls, no matter how long they'd been missing. And yet when I rang our local station at nine o'clock last night and told them that Sheridan had been missing since the afternoon I was told that they weren't interested until Sheridan had been missing for twenty-four hours. Therefore either they didn't follow your instructions or you're a liar'.

Rebecca was seething. She knew that the notice had gone out. Why had that station slipped up? Heads would fucking roll over this. As if there weren't enough bullets being loaded into the gun and pointed at her.

'I'm sorry, Mrs. Taylor' said Rebecca. 'The notice did go out and I don't know why it wasn't followed in this instance but I can assure you there'll be a formal enquiry and we will get to the bottom of it'.

'A formal enquiry? You can have all the formal enquiries you like but it won't take away my pain. You didn't know how old she was. All you knew was that she was a teenager but you didn't know if she was a minor or an adult and that should've given you an ever greater incentive to try and track her down. Do you know what it's like? Do you know what it feels like to watch the morning news and see your daughter's picture splashed across the screen? Do you know what it feels like to find out from that same news programme that she murdered someone and then died in a burned out car? Can you conceive of how that feels? Can you?'

Ellie didn't know how much more she could take. When her ex-husband Brian had betrayed her in such a brutal and public way she hadn't known a broken heart like it but she'd had to pick herself and her daughters up and start all over again. She hadn't had any choice if only for the sake of her daughters Sheridan and Paige and because she'd never been one to just give up the ghost when the going got tough. They'd moved from their dream home to somewhere that was less than ideal but she'd managed to keep the roof over their heads. She'd managed to work things out sufficiently so they could survive and continue with their lives. It had been a struggle and Sheridan had taken against everything right from the start which hadn't made things very easy. Then Ellie had taken a part time job at the nearby refugee centre which was where she met Arif. He was the epitome of tall, dark and handsome with his dark, dark eyes and jet black hair. She'd fallen for him instantly although she'd been cautious not to let it show until she was sure that he felt the same way. She brought him into her life and his charm and the beautiful way he spoke English were a hit with everyone except Sheridan. She held out even when Ellie became pregnant with Tariq. Now she had a beautiful son to go with her beautiful daughters. But still Sheridan refused to embrace any of it. She watched the anger rise up in her so unpredictably at times. She'd once hit her sister Paige and for a while Paige had refused to be alone with her big sister. And all the time Ellie's ex-husband Brian hadn't been in touch. She'd wanted him to take Sheridan for a while and see if a few weeks with her Dad might calm her down and make her more rational. If only Brian had been willing to be a responsible parent, perhaps none of this would've happened.

'Why didn't you start looking for her last night?' asked Arif. 'Who made that decision?'

'I did' said Rebecca. 'I didn't want anyone protecting Sheridan if they recognized her. Because let's not forget here that she murdered a stranger who was standing up for a man who Sheridan was abusing. Let's not forget that with all due respect'.

'I think you'd better leave' said Arif. He was holding Ellie as she sobbed.

'Where are your other children?' asked Ollie.

'Both Paige and our son Tariq are with their grandmother, Ellie's mother, in Ashton-under-Lyme. Paige, as you can imagine, is distraught about the death of her sister and in particular about the circumstances surrounding her death'.

'You'll pay' said Ellie.

'Sorry?' said Rebecca.

'Your decision led to the death of my daughter and you will pay for that' Ellie warned. 'I'll make sure of it'.

Jeff Barton was tucking into his breakfast on the flight from Hong Kong to Manchester. He'd opted for the 'English' breakfast but immediately wished he hadn't. The sausages tasted of nothing, the bacon was as dry as sticks, and the scrambled eggs were okay but not exactly moist. His son Toby had gone for the Chinese breakfast of three different types of Dim Sum and was very proudly sitting there eating it using his chopsticks. It made Jeff smile. He loved the bones of his son. Nothing and no-one would ever come between them.

'Daddy?' Toby asked.

'Yes, mate?'

'Do you think Brendan will cook Dim Sum for my breakfast when we get home?'

'Well we can ask him' said Jeff. He'd given Brendan, their live-in housekeeper and male Nanny some time off whilst they'd been away but he was due back to the house later on today. 'He could go with your Grandma to the Chinese supermarket to get them. I don't think they're that difficult to cook'.

'Or Grandma could bring them for him when she comes to see us?'

'Yes, I suppose she could' said Jeff. 'I don't think she'd mind'.

Jeff and his son Toby were returning to the UK by themselves. Jeff's late wife's parents who they'd travelled out with were staying on in China for another week. They'd had a wonderful holiday. Jeff took great delight seeing Toby soaking up his late mother Lillie Mae's Chinese heritage and he was determined that he would always do so. Lillie Mae's mother Cynthia had talked with Jeff at great length one evening. She said that she and her husband would completely understand if Jeff met someone else and wanted his life to move on. All they asked was that he'd maintain contact with them and never allow Toby to forget his Chinese heritage. Jeff had reassured her on both counts.

But he did want to finally move on with his own personal life. He'd done a lot of thinking whilst he'd been away and now understood that Rebecca Stockton could be the new woman for him. He'd treated her badly. He'd led her up the garden path and then closed the door on any future relationship. But he'd been wrong. He knew that now. So when he got back he was going to try and make it up with Rebecca and see if she would give him one more chance.

Shortly after takeoff from Hong Kong they'd lifted the armrest between their two seats, Toby being by the window and Jeff being on the aisle, and Toby had snuggled up to his Dad whilst they watched a film and played some games on the small seatback video screens. Then they'd both dropped off and now as the map on the screen showed them they were flying over Hamburg, Germany before crossing the North Sea and beginning the descent into Manchester. Just another hour or so and they'd be home and Jeff was looking forward to finding out what had been going on in his absence.

SIX

The next morning Jeff walked into a situation that if he didn't get control of would begin to threaten the integrity of his team. He'd gone into work early – a combination of jet lag not letting him sleep and an eagerness to get back to work. He took the notes on the case with him to a meeting with Chief Superintendent Chambers and then went back to the squad room where the rest of the team had arrived for work and clearly gone into a sharp row.

'I'm just saying that, on reflection, the decision perhaps wasn't the right one' DC Adrian Bradshaw insisted as he appeared to be locking horns with DI Rebecca Stockton. DC Joe Alexander was looking on but in the restless state he appeared to be in, Jeff didn't think it would be long before he waded into the battle.

'So you're saying I screwed up then, Adrian?' Rebecca demanded.

'I'm saying we all make mistakes, ma'am but Ellie Taylor on the news this morning seemed genuinely upset and angry that we seemed to have wasted those hours when we could've been out looking for her daughter'.

'So you are saying I screwed up'

'If that's how you want to take it, ma'am, but that's up to you'.

'The DI has no choice from the way you're sounding, Adrian' Joe sneered. 'So don't come all this you've chosen to take it the wrong way bullshit because that's exactly what it is'.

'And this poor wretch of a girl who everyone is falling over themselves to protect the reputation of had just murdered someone! Are you forgetting that little detail, Adrian?'

'Of course I'm not, ma'am' said Adrian in as firm a voice as he thought he could use against a senior officer. 'But it's no good us all thinking we didn't make a mistake when in my opinion we did and we missed a potential opportunity to find her alive'.

'It's easy to throw wisdom at the fire after it's been lit in the wrong place' said Joe. 'We're a team here, Adrian, and we take collective responsibility'.

'Don't you dare think you've got to remind me of the nature of teamwork, Joe' Adrian shot back. 'You know as well as I do that I've never been one to fly solo on any investigation. Whatever I've done has always been for the benefit of the team'.

Joe knew Adrian was right on that one. 'Except in the case of this argument we're having'.

'There wouldn't be an argument if you stepped back just a little and tried to understand what I'm saying'.

'You're saying I did wrong, DC Bradshaw' said Rebecca. 'Well at least I know where I stand with you'.

Jeff took great delight in taking advantage of the fact that they hadn't noticed him standing in the doorway of the squad room. 'Good grief!' he exclaimed.

It was pathetic the way their three heads swung round displaying three sets of rabbit eyes caught in the headlights. He really had to struggle not to laugh.

'Look at you lot. Can't I leave you lot for two weeks without you falling out? I've seen my son Toby and his mates act better than that and they're only six years old. Now grow up the lot of you'.

They all apologized and then wished Jeff 'welcome back' from his holidays with the broadest smiles any of them could manage after the heat of the previous moments. Rebecca then glared at Adrian. She wasn't going to forget this.

DS Ollie Wright then came in. 'Ah, Sir, welcome back' said Ollie. 'How was your trip?'

'It was wonderful Ollie, thank you' said Jeff who was glad to see Ollie hadn't been part of the circus a few moments ago. It wouldn't have been like him anyway. 'Now Ollie, I want you to look at the staff lists of the schools that Sheridan Taylor attended and see if there's anyone who taught there when she was a pupil and who subsequently ended up on the sex offenders list. See if she was ever part of any scandal. Then in a couple of hours time I want you and me to go out and see Ellie Taylor to see if we can pour some calm over troubled waters. Say about eleven?'

'That'll be fine, sir' said Ollie and went to his desk to begin trawling the lists that Jeff had requested.

Jeff then turned to Adrian and Joe. 'And if you two boys can promise to play nicely together I want every bit of CCTV in and around that warehouse where the burned out Mondeo was found. It must have been picked up by something at some point. Also, check out the most direct route between where the petrol station is in Ancoats and where the warehouse is in Cheetham Hill. It was late afternoon and it was starting to get dark. It's my guess that Sheridan Taylor was assaulted in the car and her attacker probably used the warehouse for seclusion that combined with the fading light to provide perfect cover'. He then turned to Rebecca. 'DI Stockton? My office, please'.

'I'm going to stand up for myself' said Rebecca after she'd sat down in Jeff's office. 'I'm not just going to roll over and take a bollocking'.

'Who says anything about a bollocking?'

'Well you're undermining me by taking Ollie out to see Ellie Taylor'.

'It's about damage limitation, Rebecca. You should be able to rise above it'.

'Yeah, I get that, I really do but … well I thought from your tone out there?'

'I was angry at the way you three were arguing so openly' said Jeff. 'It would've had a negative impact on the team if anybody from outside had seen it. You know how it is in this place. They love to get something on another team'.

'I know and we were being stupid' Rebecca admitted. 'Look, did you have a good holiday?'

'Yes, I did' said Jeff. 'We were spoilt rotten by all of Lillie Mae's family as you can imagine and Toby especially was made a huge fuss of wherever we went' He patted his stomach. 'I've put on a bit of weight too. Every day there was so much food prepared for us'.

'That won't do you any harm' said Rebecca. 'You were too thin anyway'.

It was that rare moment when something personal passed between them. Jeff liked the way that Rebecca's auburn hair dangled around her shoulders and she looked good. Whilst he was away he realised what a damn fool he'd been. It wasn't that he didn't find her attractive. He'd always found Rebecca attractive. It was just that he hadn't been able to find a way to step into the future without Lillie Mae. Maybe it was when Lillie Mae's mother had basically given him her blessing for him to move on with his personal life and find someone to spend the rest of his days with.

'There's no sign of that stress having got to you' said Jeff.

'Do you think I made the wrong decision, Jeff?' Rebecca asked. 'I need to know'.

Jeff pondered the question for a few moments and tried to see how it would go with the conversation he really wanted to have with Rebecca about their personal lives and whether or not they could be joined up after all.

'You do, don't you? I can tell by the look on your face'.

'I didn't say that, Becky'.

'No but it's written all over your face that you side with Adrian Bradshaw'.

'I think you took a risk that this time didn't pay off'.

'Would you have taken it too?'

'Maybe I would, yes' said Jeff. 'But look Becky, you've got to toughen up on this one. All of us have taken decisions that we've regretted afterwards but it doesn't mean we're bad police officers. Don't shy away from it. Learn from it. Otherwise if you're seen to get a bit tetchy and sensitive over decisions you make that don't end up going your way then believe me the glittering career that I know is yours will be sure to fade'.

'Oh I know' said Rebecca. 'I've already had a similar warning from Chief Superintendent Chambers. She said that if I started acting like a maverick it wouldn't go down well with the hierarchy'.

'And she's right' said Jeff. 'But you didn't act like a maverick. You made a decision that could've gone either way but you'll have to live with the way it did go.

'Thanks, Jeff ' said Rebecca. 'But how's it going to look when you turn up at Ellie Taylor's place with Ollie wanting to calm troubled waters as you said?'

'She needs reassurance, that's all' said Jeff. 'Like I said before Becky we've all been there and if someone hasn't then they're not a particularly good police officer'.

'Okay' said Rebecca. 'So what do you want me to do now in terms of the investigation? I mean, now that you're back and are the senior investigating officer'.

'I want you to go with DC Bradshaw and follow up on whatever he and DC Alexander find from the CCTV footage'.

Rebecca smiled wryly. 'Mend my fences with Adrian'.

'I think it's necessary, don't you?'

'Aw, look I don't have anything against Adrian'.

'Really?'

'Okay I'm lying' Rebecca admitted. 'But it'll pass. I'll do as you say, Jeff, and I promise I'll be good'.

'Okay' said Jeff. 'There is something else I need to talk to you about. Rebecca, I know I've messed you about in terms of our personal lives and … '

' … ah look, Jeff that's all water under the bridge and there's no hard feelings on my side'.

'I'm glad to hear that because you see, whilst I was away I kind of came to my senses as far as you and I are concerned and … well I want to know if you will give me another chance?'

Rebecca couldn't believe what she was hearing. She'd waited so long to hear this from him but it was too late. And in facing that she understood how she could disappoint him the way he had disappointed her all this time.

'Jeff, I've started seeing Joe Alexander'.

Jeff was shocked. 'This is new'.

'It is' said Rebecca who was feeling very uncomfortable.

'I really can't turn my back for five minutes' said Jeff trying his best to make light of the blow he'd received. 'Well I wish you and Joe all the best'.

'Do you mean that?'

'Yes, I do' said Jeff. 'I hesitated for too long. I led you on a bit and then let you down'.

'I'm sorry, Jeff'.

'Don't be sorry' said Jeff. 'Just have yourselves a good time and be happy'.

SEVEN

He was used to cries of pain. They were his currency. It had always been the way he'd got through every long, lonely year. It was like listening to the cries of saints. Heaven must feel like that. Not that he was ever going to find out.

But Sheridan had been something else. She'd gone too far. She'd crossed the line from being a victim to being a fucking nuisance. Hadn't he groomed her well? It was true that she was at the higher age range of the girls he and his friends liked to entertain but that didn't matter because she looked younger. And she'd been easy to impress. She'd been positively begging to let him have his way. But he'd been saving her. He'd been waiting for her to make it to sixteen so that he could go way back in time and remember what it felt like to fuck a girl who wasn't underage. Sheridan was a special girl alright. That's why he'd followed her that afternoon across the patch of waste ground and up to the petrol station. He'd intended to approach her when she was walking home but the stupid little bitch had gone and murdered some bloke. He had to give her a way out then. He had to rescue her. He had to make sure that she needed him.

'What are you going to do?' she'd asked as they headed round the Mancunian way motorway and then he took the turning that would take them into North Manchester.

'Don't worry, you'll be alright'.

'I want to know where we're going'.

'I said don't worry'.

'Where are we going?' she screamed.

'Do you want to be safe or don't you?'

'I want to go home' she said and then started to cry. 'I want my Mum'.

'But she's with that darkie and they've got a kid together. She doesn't want you anymore. Your nose has been well and truly pushed out of joint my girl and that's why you need me'.

'Take me back to my Mum, please'.

She was such an ungrateful little cow. He'd just saved her from having to face the police on a murder charge. Didn't that matter to her? Didn't she think that might inspire just a little bit of gratitude? He placed his hand on her knee.

'I hate to see you so upset' he said. 'Your Mum can't get you out of this'.

'If you let me go now I won't say anything, alright?'

'Let you go? Let you go where? A young girl as beautiful as you shouldn't be out on her own at night'.

'Let me go!'

'You know I can't do that, Sheridan'.

EIGHT

'I'm not here to make any judgments on anyone, Mrs. Taylor' said Jeff who was sitting with DS Ollie Wright in the living room of Ellie Taylor's house.

'I see' said Ellie.

'I just want to know what happened to your daughter last Sunday' Jeff went on. 'It's my job to find out and I don't think you've started off with a very good impression of us'.

'That's an understatement'.

'Then let me try and engage with you so we can get justice for all concerned'.

Ellie heard those words 'justice for all concerned' and couldn't help but start to cry. Her daughter had been murdered. But on the way she'd murdered an innocent man over some stupid argument. Her little girl had taken a knife to a man who'd now left behind two little kids. It wasn't just the anger over the police delay in trying to find Sheridan that night that was getting to her. It was the crushing reality of knowing what Sheridan had done to an innocent man called Sam Jackson.

'We'll give you some time, Mrs. Taylor' said Jeff.

'It doesn't matter' said Ellie. She wiped her eyes with a tissue. 'I've never been one for pushing things to one side. I like to face them head on. I think that ultimately you're better off doing that'.

Jeff admired this woman for her strength and her certainty in this time of such great sadness and loss. 'Wise words Mrs. Taylor and admirable, if I may say, in the circumstances'.

'I'm not looking for plaudits, detective' said Ellie. 'But it is hard at the moment. It's devastated our family. I have a new baby as you know, my little son Tariq. He's upstairs sleeping at the moment. He'll never know his big sister even though she didn't want to know him for the short time she knew him'.

'Why was that, Mrs. Taylor?'

'Because she didn't like the fact that he was brown' said Ellie. 'Sheridan had somehow got it into her head that it was okay to be racist. Where she got that from I really don't know but I guess it was because of my partner Arif who's from Iraq. Even though my ex husband left me and left me penniless, Sheridan always believed that I was the bad guy and held out the hope that her father would come back. I tried time and again to explain to her that he would never be back but she always accused me of lying. Arif is a really decent human being and has tried so hard to reach out to Sheridan. But she wouldn't have any of it and I think the whole race thing was her way of fighting Arif's presence in our lives and her father's absense'.

'These kind of things are hard to take in families'.

'You know what I'm talking about?'

'My late wife was Chinese and I have a son who my parents have rejected because he's mixed race. So yes, I do know what it feels like and I don't have any contact with my parents because of it'.

Ollie had never heard his boss talk so frankly and openly about his personal life before and he didn't know about what Jeff had revealed. It was sad and deplorable on the part of Jeff's parents. But he'd used his own personal situation to try and make some kind of common ground with Ellie Taylor and for that he got top marks from Ollie.

'Mrs. Taylor' Ollie began. 'We need to find out who was driving that Mondeo. Do you know of anyone who you daughter would've known sufficiently to get into a car with them? Think hard and however unlikely you think something might be it may lead to us finding some answers. Just the name of someone would give us a start'.

Ellie looked down slightly. 'No, no there isn't anyone I can think of'.

She's lying, thought Jeff.

'Are you sure, Mrs. Taylor? Are you sure there's nobody you can think of who we might want to talk to?'

'No' said Ellie. 'Absolutely nobody'.

Why is she lying? Is she trying to protect someone?

'Right' said Jeff. 'Well we'll need to interview Arif Rashid. It's standard procedure to be able to eliminate him from our enquiries'.

'Yes, I thought that would be the case' said Ellie. 'Well Arif does two jobs with two different office cleaning companies in order to contribute to the family finances. I'll give you the details. He was a doctor in Iraq but they won't let him practise here. I think it's disgraceful'.

'May I ask if you had any other relationships between the time your husband left and meeting Arif?' Ollie probed as gently as he could.

'No' said Ellie. 'There's been nobody else'.

Jeff and Ollie sat outside in Jeff's car for a few moments to discuss the interview with Ellie Taylor.

'She's lying, Sir' said Ollie.

'Of course she is' Jeff agreed. 'There is someone who she knows we might need to talk to but why is she protecting them? Why would she want to protect the potential murderer of her daughter?'

'There could be all kinds of reasons if it's wrapped up in her personal life, Sir' said Ollie who liked DI Rebecca Stockton very much but he was so glad that Jeff Barton was back. It was like a grown up was back in charge. 'I'd say an ex boyfriend though'.

'Yes, so would I' said Jeff. 'So how are we going to get her to open up about him? In the meantime I take it no house to house has been done around here?'

'No, Sir' said Ollie who was almost embarrassed to admit that.

'Well let's get it started. Somebody might've seen the Mondeo and who was driving it'.

'Okay, Sir'.

'And I want house to house conducted around the petrol station too for the same reason. Somebody has to have seen that bloody car'.

'My brother calls it the end of fun car' said Ollie.

'What, the Mondeo? Why?'

'Well it's what men with families have to get' said Ollie. 'My brother had a sports convertible before he and his wife had the kids. I think he thought he'd traded in his youth when he traded it in for the Mondeo'.

Jeff laughed. 'Well thankfully I kept hold of my Audi and as it doesn't look like I'll be having anymore kids in the foreseeable future I think I'll continue to keep hold of it'.

'You do that, Sir' said Ollie, looking round Jeff's car which was in impeccable condition. He really did take care of it. 'The Audi is a mighty fine motor'.

'I don't think you can beat German cars to be honest' said Jeff who then stretched and yawned. 'Don't take it personally, Ollie. I'm not bored with your company. But I think part of me is still in Hong Kong'.

Ollie laughed. 'No worries, Sir. I always get jet lag when I go back to see my relatives in Jamaica. Not that I've gone back for a while which disappoints my Mum and Dad'.

'You can't live your life for your Mum and Dad, Ollie. You've got to find your own way and you seem to be doing alright'.

'Yeah, I've no complaints' Ollie agreed. 'I'm still close to my Mum and Dad though, Sir. They even accepted the fact that I'm gay and I live with my partner Neil and the Caribbean community isn't always accepting of same sex relationships. I feel lucky which is why I was sad to hear about your situation with your parents, Sir. That's if I'm not speaking out of turn?'

'You know me well enough by now, Ollie' said Jeff. 'You can say what you like to me. As for my parents … well it may mend itself one day. Who knows? I certainly didn't cause the rift. They did because they objected to me marrying a Chinese girl and they now take that out on my son. It's so fundamental and I've been so angry and hurt by it that I don't know if it ever could be mended to be honest'.

They were both shaken out of their conversation by a sharp tapping at the window on Ollie's side. He wound the window down. A woman who they both put in her sixties wearing a light blue raincoat over a white blouse and dark blue trousers leaned her head down to speak to them.

'Are you the police officers looking after our Sheridan's case?'

'Yes?' said Ollie who then introduced himself and Jeff.

'Forgive me. I was walking down the road and I saw you coming out of my daughter's house. With the way you're dressed I put two and two together. I'm Sheridan's grandmother. My name is Joan Sanders. Ellie Taylor is my daughter and though it grieves me to tell you there's something you should know that I know she won't have told you. Can I come down to the station? I'd rather talk there than round here'.

'Are you ready now, Mrs. Saunders?' said Jeff.

'Yes' she replied. 'I am. I was on my way to my daughter's but I haven't knocked on the door yet'.

'Then jump in the back and let's go' said Jeff. 'There's a burger type takeaway place just down the road with parking. We'll talk there over a coffee and then I'll run you back here'.

The three of them sat round a half circle table on red plastic covered seating with their piping hot coffee in polystyrene cups. Ollie clearly didn't come into places like this and his slightly uncomfortable pose made Jeff smile. He on the other hand had been in this sort of family orientated eating place many times with Toby and Toby's mates. Kids love this kind of food although he rationed Toby's indulgence of it. He didn't want him ever to make fast food his first choice. Joan looked at peace with her surroundings. No doubt she came in here with her grandchildren.

'So what is it you think your daughter hasn't told us, Mrs. Sanders?' asked Jeff whilst sipping his coffee. The caffeine would be useful to shake off the lethargy that was beginning to creep through his body.

'This is hard for me' said Joan. 'I don't like going behind my daughter's back but there's so much at stake here that I have to try and put those feelings to one side and do the right thing'.

'Which is?' asked Jeff.

'When Arif came into my daughter's life I was immediately impressed by him' Joan began. 'He seemed to really love my daughter and she'd been so badly let down and scarred by what her ex-husband had done to her. If I was driving a car and he stepped into the road in front of me I'd be so tempted to put my foot on the accelerator although perhaps I shouldn't tell you gentlemen that. But he left her almost destitute. I had to clean out my own savings to get her and the girls back on their feet'.

'So what happened with Arif, Mrs. Sanders?' Ollie asked.

'Nothing that was bad' Joan insisted. 'He moved in and a few weeks later my daughter was pregnant. I didn't see any wrong in any of it. My granddaughter Paige was thrilled at the prospect of a new half brother or sister. She liked Arif just like we all did'.

'But what are you trying to tell us, Mrs. Sanders?' Jeff wanted to know.

'Well nothing went wrong with Arif' Joan emphasized. 'He's not the problem here. No, the problem was that Sheridan just wouldn't accept that her mother had moved on from her father and was now with Arif to the extent that she was now pregnant by him. She became bad tempered, she answered her mother back and said some terrible things and she sucked all the happiness out of what her mother had found with Arif. It was a happy time and yet it was a dreadful time. Sheridan was so full of anger and spite. I'd never seen her like that. It was as if she just wanted to hit out at the entire world. It was such a worrying time for Ellie and although she had Arif I know there was someone else she also came to rely on'.

'Who was that?' Jeff asked.

'He was a teacher at Sheridan's school' said Joan. 'Sheridan seemed to grow close to him and we thought that if she had someone she could confide in then it might help. Ellie met him a few times and she came to rely on him. He seemed like a good sort'.

'How do you mean he seemed like a good sort?' Ollie questioned. 'Did something happen to make you change your mind?'

Joan hesitated. Sometimes the truth was really hard to tell. 'I came round to the house one Thursday afternoon. He was lying on top of Sheridan's bed whilst she was inside it wearing not very much and I didn't think it was appropriate so I told him to leave. I mean, why would he want to do that unless he had some kind of ulterior motive? My daughter Ellie didn't do anything about it because she just didn't see any wrong in him. She thought he was misunderstood but Arif, to his great credit, insisted that he never came to the house again'.

'And what was this man's name?' Jeff wanted to know.

'His name was Leo McKenzie ' Joan revealed. 'And he's still in post at Sheridan's school'.

When they got back to the station DC Joe Alexander was the only one there in the squad room.

'Where is everyone, Joe?' asked Jeff. He didn't hold anything against Joe for having jumped in there with Rebecca. He was certainly more grown up than that and besides, if he hadn't hesitated for all those weeks and months instead of acting on what he could see clearly written all over Rebecca's face then Joe wouldn't have stood a chance. He knew he'd only got himself to blame.

'DI Stockton and DS Bradshaw have gone out to follow up on a call we received about an hour ago from someone who lives over the road from the petrol station' Joe explained. 'He says he saw two men get out of the Mondeo when it parked at the petrol station but that one of them then walked off'.

'Walked off?'

'In the direction of the city centre apparently' Joe went on. 'The man who rang up said he could give a full description. He was cleaning his windows at the time apparently and got a pretty good view'.

'But why would he just walk off?'

'Who can say at this point, Sir' said Joe. 'A sudden attack of conscience and he no longer wanted to be a part of what was going on? Possibly but not likely in my opinion, Sir, but perhaps more importantly right now is that we got the registration number of the Mondeo on some CCTV footage from a set of traffic lights further back along Stockport Road. I ran it through the system and it's registered to Farndale Motors of Littleborough. I've checked them out. They're a small garage who also hire out cars but the interesting thing here is that they vow and declare that the Mondeo was not hired out to anyone last Sunday afternoon. They were closed then and as far as they're concerned it was sitting on their premises'.

'So why didn't they report it missing?'

'I spoke to a Liam Nightingale. He says he's the son of the owner and he's in charge of the place whilst his parents are away on holiday in Florida. When I pressed him on why he didn't report the car as missing he said he didn't realise it was'.

'Do you detect the smell of bullshit, Joe?'

'Very strongly, Sir'.

'Right, well we'll wait for everyone to come back and then we'll go over what we've got so far. But there are two people we definitely need to speak to urgently. One is Liam Nightingale and the other is Mr. Leo McKenzie'.

NINE

Hayley Adams had always been a particularly needy child. She absolutely had to have one hundred and ten percent of your attention or else she thought you didn't want her around. It sorely tested her mother's patience at times. Jeanette Adams would have to admit that although she loved her daughter she wasn't always very easy to like. Hayley was now thirteen and there was still at least one episode of tears every single day. Jeanette's son Stefan was completely different. He was just two years older than his sister but Jeanette could rely on him to take care of his own breakfast if she was running short of time and she didn't really need to worry about him at all. He was self-confident and able to act like the young man that he was.

But Jeanette was worried about Hayley in another way. Jeanette had now been divorced from her ex-husband Steve for two years and Hayley hadn't adjusted to her parents being divorced at all. It had been the cause of all her tears since it happened because she'd got it into her head that her Dad and her Dad's family had rejected her.

'And yet far from it' Jeanette insisted. 'My ex in-laws have gone out of their way to make her feel as much a part of their family as before but she just won't have it and then we get these tears and tears and more tears. I've tried my best to understand. I've tried my best to sit down and talk to her just her and me. Her Dad has sat her down, her grandparents have sat her down and tried to reassure her. But none of us are getting anywhere. My ex husband has Hayley and Stefan every other weekend and at least one night a week but those visits are always on a knife edge because the slightest thing goes wrong and she starts crying and tells my ex that he doesn't want her. It's starting to affect Stefan now too because of course her constant tears are having an impact on his visits to his Dad and he hardly speaks to Hayley now because he's simply had enough of her behaviour. I don't know what to do anymore'.

'I can see it must be exhausting' said Leo McKenzie. He was Hayley's form teacher at school and Jeanette wanted him to keep an eye on Hayley who'd got herself a boyfriend in her class called Craig. That's why she'd come into school for a meeting with Leo who she'd met several times before on parents' evenings. 'What's your worry with regard to Craig?'

'She thinks that she can replace all the love that she thinks she's lost by having a baby' Jeanette explained. 'And I'm worried sick that she'll use Craig to get herself pregnant'.

'Ah, I see' said Leo.

'Craig is a sensible lad and I know his parents' said Jeanette. 'But a lad who's newly full of testosterone and a girl who may be only too willing to take some of it off him ... well I don't need to spell it out, do I?'

'No, you don't' said Leo. 'But tell me, if you could be completely honest with Hayley and say to her whatever you felt like then what would that be?'

Jeanette paused. Not because she didn't know what she'd say but because of how harsh it would sound.

'I'd want to say 'oh come on you selfish little madam, it's not all about you and you've got to grow up and get on with it like your brother has'.

'I can understand all of that, yep'.

'I'm really sorry to land all of this on you this week, Leo, after all this terrible business about Sheridan Taylor. You used to teach her I understand?'

'Yes I did' said Leo as neutrally as he could. 'And her sister Paige is in my class now as you know'.

'To be burned alive in that car' said Jeanette who then shivered. 'The poor girl. Her poor mother as well. Have you spoken to the family?'

'No' said Leo who'd been sweating like a bloody pig these past few nights, wondering and waiting for the police to knock at his door. However many reassurances he received he'd still have to go through some kind of process and he wasn't looking forward to that. Life shouldn't have turned out this way. It's certainly not how he'd always imagined it would be. But it has turned out this way and he just had to deal with it. 'I won't approach the family until the dust has settled a bit. It's not appropriate to go in there interfering at this time. I mean, they also have to face up to the fact that Sheridan murdered an innocent man at the petrol station'.

'I know' said Jeanette. 'But, and I'm not trying to excuse it, but that must've been a heat of the moment type of thing, sad as it is for the man's family. But to set alight to a car with a young girl in it … no, that was a deliberate act and he should be strung up for it'.

'Well, look leave it with me about Hayley. I'll have a chat to her and to Craig and see what the score is'

'Thank you, Leo, I really appreciate it' said Jeanette. 'But I'd better get back to work now. You really are a very special teacher, you know. The school and the kids are lucky to have you'.

Leo smiled. 'I do my best'.

'You rang, me lady?' said Jeff when he arrived at June Hawkins pathology lab where she examining the remains of Sheridan Taylor on the usual long steel table.

June looked up from the job in hand and paused for a moment. 'Oh Jeff, I was just having a fantasy that you were Parker to my Lady Penelope'.

Jeff laughed. 'You are naughty'.

'Well I'm not darling because you never give me the chance'.

'At least you haven't got Bon Jovi blasting out of your speakers today' said Jeff noting the quiet calm of the lab compared to how it normally is.

'Well that's because Jon Bon Jovi has effectively ditched Richie Sambora'.

'Is Sambora the guitarist?'

'Correct' said June. 'He was the backbone of the band and just because he didn't want to go on tour at the same time as Jon Bon Jovi did Jon Bon Jovi ditched him. So I'm boycotting the band in support of Richie. And in any case, the last album was shite'.

'Good, well I'm glad we've got that cleared up' said Jeff. 'And there was I about to go and find a room where paint was drying. So, why have you brought me down here?'

June had been examining the body of Sheridan Taylor. It hadn't all been burnt to a cinder and there was enough burned flesh left for June to have made some interesting discoveries.

'She was pregnant' June declared.

'What?'

'You know, that condition women have when they're carrying a baby?'

'Yes thank you Doctor I do know' said Jeff, smiling. 'I don't know why I'm just surprised, that's all'.

'You mean you didn't think that nice girls from nice families open their legs with as much apparent enthusiasm as girls from an estate?'

'Shut up!'

'Sorry' said June, laughing. 'I was only teasing and it was worth it to see the look on your face'.

'Yes well you've had your fun at my expense' said Jeff. 'Now let's get down to business'.

June would love to get down to anything with Jeff Barton but sadly he'd proved immune to her charms. Perhaps it was a good job. She wasn't that good with kids and he was very close to his little boy.

'Yes but what's really interesting for you is that she was certainly sexually assaulted and the DNA from that doesn't match the DNA from the foetus'.

'So whoever assaulted her that night wasn't the father of her baby?'

'Correct'.

'How far gone was she?'

'It is a guess but I'd say about four months, maybe five. There isn't a large bump so I don't think she could've been showing. But still, I guess it would be interesting to see if her mother knew'.

Jeff gathered the team together around the white board in the squad room. He'd just come from a blazing row with Chief Superintendent Chambers during which she'd repeated her previous insistence to DI Rebecca Stockton that there would be no extra resources available for the investigation. He thought that Chambers might have changed her mind given the emerging complexity of just what they were finding out but it had been a surefire resounding non-negotiable no. Jeff hadn't been able to stop himself from seeing red. He just couldn't figure out why an investigation like this one wouldn't take priority over others. They were all in the office first thing every morning and all stayed well into the evening. He didn't want to think where Rebecca and Joe went to spend what remained of the day but Adrian had children to go home for, just like Jeff had Toby to go home for and Ollie had his partner. They should've interviewed Sheridan Taylor's father and her step-father Arif. They both had alibis. Her father was in Spain and Arif was out with her mother. But still they should've had a more intense talk with Arif, not that Jeff suspected him of anything, but just as a matter of routine. Developments and discoveries had overtaken routine like they do on most investigations. That's when you rely on getting more resources to follow things up.

'Okay then everyone' said Jeff. 'First of all I know we're all getting pushed to the limits on this and you're not seeing enough of the people who really matter to you. I'm sorry about that. I have asked for extra resources but I'm afraid to say my request has been turned down'.

'Turned down, Sir?' DS Adrian Bradshaw questioned.

'I know' said Jeff. 'It's hard to believe, Adrian. But that's where we are. Both DI Stockton and myself have made the request and we've both been turned down'.

'It doesn't seem right, Sir' said DS Joe Alexander.

'No it doesn't, Joe' said Jeff who was pissed off that he was having to expect so much from his team that wouldn't be expected of other teams fighting different types of crime. He was irritated by the stance of Chief Superintendent Chambers. What the fuck was she thinking? 'But like I said, it's where we are and we've got to get on with it. Now, this case started off with Sheridan Taylor taking out a knife in a petrol station and fatally stabbing Sam Jackson who'd intervened on behalf of the counter assistant who Sheridan was verbally abusing. In a panic she runs out onto the forecourt and straight into a purposely waiting Ford Mondeo. She knew the driver. But what also matters to us is that a witness living across the road saw the Mondeo drive up to the petrol station and he says there were two men in it, one younger, one older. The younger of the two got out of the car and walked off in the direction of the city centre. Why?'

As Jeff goes through everything on the board he uses the marker pen to point at the relevant maps, photos, and names. It's something he's done a hundred times before but in this instance he feels like they could be getting close to something. They just needed to join up a couple more dots.

'Later on that same evening the car is found burned out behind a warehouse in Cheetham Hill with Sheridan's body inside. We now know from June Hawkins that Sheridan was pregnant but by whom? Was it the driver of the Mondeo? Is that how she recognized him and got in without any objection? No, because June also confirms that Sheridan was sexually assaulted in the Mondeo before the driver set it on fire whilst she was still in it and that the DNA of that is different to the DNA of the foetus that had been growing inside Sheridan. So did the driver know she was pregnant? Did he know who the father was?'

'Then there's the Mondeo itself. Registered to a small, family run garage and car hire company in Littleborough. Being looked after by the son of the owner at the moment who says he didn't notice the car was missing. DS Wright? I'd like you to take DS Bradshaw with you to see Mr. Liam Nightingale straight after this briefing to press him on the ridiculous responses he's given to our questions so far. Depending on the answers he gives us I believe he'll lead us to this man, Leo McKenzie'.

'McKenzie is a teacher at Sheridan's school. Now according to Sheridan's Grandmother, Sheridan's mother Ellie Taylor came home to find McKenzie lying on top of Sheridan's bed and Sheridan was in it. We will need to re-interview her on the basis of this new information and I'll be taking care of that with DI Stockton'.

'Is it your thinking, Sir, that Leo McKenzie is the father of Sheridan's baby?' asked Ollie Wright.

'That's exactly what I'm thinking, Ollie'.

'But I take it that Ellie Taylor didn't report McKenzie for being caught in a compromising position with her daughter?' Rebecca questioned.

'Correct, DI Stockton' said Jeff.

'So why didn't she?'

'According to her mother Ellie Taylor wanted to give McKenzie the benefit of the doubt because he'd been good to her and her family since they'd had to uproot themselves from the posh end of Greater Manchester to a not so salubrious area after her husband had gone off and left her bankrupt'.

'That's some benefit of the bloody doubt, Sir' said Rebecca. 'Finding your daughter's teacher in her bedroom'.

'There'd be no benefit of the doubt if that happened to me and one of my daughters' said DC Adrian Bradshaw. 'Nor my son for that matter. What was this Ellie Taylor woman thinking for God's sake?'

'That's what we need to find out, Adrian' said Jeff. 'And I admit it does sound pretty incredulous. Now, DS Alexander?'

'Sir?' said Joe who'd been wondering when the boss would get to him. 'Now I want you to go down to see our witness across the road from the petrol station. Take this picture of Leo McKenzie with you that we downloaded from the website of Sheridan's school where he teaches. I reckon he'll say it's him who he saw walking away from the Mondeo last Sunday afternoon. Well that's it for now everyone. All I need is five minutes to down a cup of strong black coffee to stave off the continuing jet lag'.

TEN

Hayley Adams was walking down the street about a block away from her home. She was in tears. It was her usual state. Her Mum just didn't understand. All she wanted was a baby to replace all the love that she'd lost when her father left. Why was that so hard for everybody to understand? Why couldn't she get it through to them all? She wanted the love. She wanted the baby because it would be totally dependent on her.

She was going out to meet him. She'd done it before. Only once but ever since her teacher Leo McKenzie took her to one side one morning when she came into school all upset she'd known about him. He was the only one who seemed to understand. He held her so tight that night and he never got on to her about anything. He made her feel safe and warm. He gave her drinks and chocolate and said that next time they'd have themselves a party. He provided her with a place to go when nobody she knew understood.

He drove up alongside her and she smiled when she realised it was him.

'How are you princess?' he asked after they'd driven off.

Hayley started crying again. 'I hate my life. I hate the way my Mum is making me feel'.

'It's not fair, love' he said, softly. 'But tonight you can forget all that because you don't need to be upset. Just for a few hours whilst you're with me you can smile again and be yourself. I promised you we'd have a little party and that's what we will have' He reached over and stroked her face gently. 'I'll take those tears away. You'll see'.

When they got to the house on the other side of town Hayley happily got out of the car and ran inside with him. He was about the same height as her Dad and he reminded her of him in some ways. He gave her a drink of coke. It tasted a bit strange but not unpleasant and she carried on drinking it. It made her feel happy. It made her not want to cry anymore. It made her feel able to talk and say so many things. It made her feel relaxed and a little tired.

'Why don't you come upstairs?' he said. He'd taken off his jacket. His shirt sleeves were undone. He held out his hand. 'Come on. We'll have ourselves a little nap'.

'I'll have to get back to my Mum's'.

'And you will' he said. 'Once you've closed your eyes for a little while. You know what she's like? If she thought you've had some fun she'll never let you out again'.

She went up the stairs with him right behind her. He gently steered her into the bedroom where she lay down on the big bed. He gave her some more of the coke with the strange taste but he didn't sit down with her.

The last thing she remembered seeing before passing out was a whole load of other men coming into the room. .

ELEVEN

'So how's things going at home?' asked DS Ollie Wright as he drove him and DC Adrian Bradshaw out to Littleborough to interview Liam Nightingale at Farndale Motors. They were on the dualcarriageway going up towards Oldham which they would have to drive through to get to Littleborough on the edge of the Moors. 'After all the traumas of last year I mean?'

'Well yeah, it was tough initially' said Adrian. 'But now we're a really tight little four-way unit and it feels good. I'm certainly not going in for any relationships in the foreseeable future. Oh no. They're off limits for now'.

'And what about meaningless sex? Doesn't Daddy want to indulge in any of that either?'

Adrian smiled and shifted in his seat. Not many people knew about his bisexuality and those that did tended to be his ex male lovers. He and Ollie had enjoyed a torrid affair a few months back which had only ended when it had become too ordinary and regular and boring. Ollie was never going to leave his partner Neil and Adrian didn't want to settle down with another man. They didn't want to get tied down by expectations.

'Are you offering your services?'

'Why not? We worked well together before if you remember?'

'Oh I remember alright' said Adrian who could feel himself getting hard at the memory of those times he spent with Ollie. 'Maybe once this case is over? Everything is a bit full on at the minute'.

'Are you holding out on me?'

'Ollie, I would like nothing more than to repeat those hot times we had' said Adrian. 'And it's nothing about you but I'm just being very cautious with my personal life at the moment. That whole business with Kate Branning scared me, Ollie. She almost killed my daughter. If she'd been able to go through with that I don't know how I would've come back from it. You understand?'

'Of course I do' said Ollie. 'But I'll be there when you change your mind'.

When they got to Farndale Motors it was just off the main road leading out of Littleborough and across the moors. The garage was attached to the showroom and there was the usual display of second hand cars for sale along with details of the car hire side of the business on a billboard attached to a pole at the entrance. Ollie drove onto the drive along the side of the showroom where they could see a door with 'office' marked on it. They figured that would be the place to find Liam Nightingale.

Inside was one of those old fashioned counters about chest height and sat at one of the desks behind typing into a computer was a girl probably in her early twenties. She was a big girl and could barely make it through the gap between the two desks after she'd stood up to come and greet them. They held up their warrant cards and introduced themselves. At that point they heard a commotion coming from what they could see was a small private office to the side of the counter and they quickly understood what was going on. Liam Nightingale was making a run for it.

Both Ollie and Adrian were quick to give chase and it only took a few seconds before they caught up with Nightingale and apprehended him.

'Right' said Ollie who was holding Nightingale firmly by the upper arm after he'd cuffed him. 'You've just earned yourself a trip to the police station, my friend'.

When Jeff got to the home of Ellie Taylor with DI Rebecca Stockton they found her knee deep in washing baby clothes.

'I use disposable nappies' said Ellie. 'But I think most people do these days, don't they?'

'We did with my son' said Jeff.

'Mrs. Taylor, why didn't you tell us about your daughter Sheridan's relationship with her teacher Leo McKenzie?'

Ellie Taylor slumped down on a chair at the kitchen table and gestured for Jeff and Rebecca to do the same. 'Yes, my mother told me she'd been to see you. I don't blame her. It's what I should've done. You see, I honestly thought that it was an innocent relationship. I'm a stupid middle class girl thrust into a world of God knows what and Leo just seemed like a bright light in an otherwise sometimes dark and dismal world'.

Rebecca was struggling to have any sympathy with the daft bitch. She probably had a baby with someone of a different race to make some kind of nauseating middle class anti racist statement. God she couldn't stand her.

'I knew she was going out and meeting Leo but the thing is she was being so damn difficult at home and Leo seemed to be able to calm her down even for a short time. He made her easier to live with for a while. I turned a blind eye to it because it made my life easier'.

'Mrs. Taylor, did you know she was pregnant?' Jeff asked.

The news clearly came as a massive shock to Ellie Taylor. They watched her face crumble into a blinding picture of pain and then she broke down and wept. When she lifted her head she couldn't help but notice the look on Rebecca's face despite all the tears.

'Don't you dare judge me' Ellie warned.

'I'm not judging you, Mrs. Taylor'.

'You're a liar! You're lying to me again! You were the one whose sheer incompetence led to my daughter being murdered by whoever that maniac was so you can get out!'

'Mrs. Taylor, we need to calm down here' said Jeff. 'Having a go at my colleague will get you nowhere'.

'Shut up! I am breaking up with grief over my daughter and you've got the nerve to look at me the way you are doing now? Get out! Get out the pair of you! You make me sick just to look at you'.

'Why did you let her throw us out of there with a flea in our ear?' Rebecca demanded once she and Jeff had got to the car.

'Because there wasn't any point in carrying on trying to talk to her in that state' said Jeff. 'And I'm surprised that you think we should've carried on a heated discussion with a woman who's just found out that her murdered daughter was pregnant!'

'Oh well maybe you think I'm incompetent too?'

'Becky, we've been through this' Jeff pleaded.

'But it's still there, isn't it? Just like it's there between us because I'm going out with Joe Alexander now. And by the way, Joe and I are getting on just fine, thank you. In fact, we're talking about going on holiday together once this case is done'.

'I'm very happy for you but now can we get back to the case which was almost completely blown off course by you not instigating that search last Sunday night'.

'Oh, so it's all coming out now then. You blame me for everything that's gone wrong in this investigation?'

'I blame you for not getting things started earlier, Becky. It has nothing to do with any personal situations. I am happy for you as far as Joe is concerned, Becky'.

'You could've fooled me'.

'But when it comes to the investigation then if you could just stand back and see the bigger picture here you'd see that you do have a case to answer for when the official enquiry takes place. A small case, a case that can be dealt with and I will back you all the way but you really need to understand how we got to this point. Now get in the car DI Stockton and let's get back to trying to solve this case'.

'So come on, Liam' said DS Ollie Wright. 'Why did you think you could get away with telling such a whopper of a lie? You were responsible for your parents' business and yet you didn't know a Ford Mondeo had gone missing?'

Liam Nightingale sat with his hands on his lap. He was folding his fingers over and over and his family solicitor was sitting beside him. He was still in his suit from work and still had his tie on. He was one of those lads who looked like he'd scrubbed himself to within an inch of his life. He was cute enough in a boring, predictable, unadventurous sort of way. Ollie wondered if he was fucking the fat girl behind reception at the showroom. If he was then she'd no doubt soon be pregnant and then she'd achieve her goal of marrying the boss's son which means she wouldn't have to think anymore about going to work for a living.

'It was a favour for a mate'

'A mate?' Ollie questioned. 'Who might that be?'

Liam looked up at his solicitor and then said 'No comment'.

'Was it Leo McKenzie, Liam?'

Liam sat up straight and then leaned forward again. He repeated the action several times. He was clearly distracted by everything that was happening and he didn't like being on the spot.

'Look Liam, we know you and Leo both live in Littleborough' said Ollie. 'Do you drink in the same pub? Are you mates that way?'

'Come on now Liam you're not helping yourself here' said Adrian. 'But you could do if you opened up to us. Some serious crimes have been committed and you're implicated in them because somehow someone got hold of a Mondeo from your yard. Now how did that happen, Liam?'

Liam shook his head.

'Have you got a girlfriend, Liam?' Ollie asked.

'Tracy behind reception is my girlfriend'.

I knew it, thought Ollie. 'Do you prefer younger girls though?'

'What do you mean?'

'What I said' said Ollie. 'Do you like young girls who are underage? Is that how you get your sexual kicks?'

'No!' said Liam, emphatically. 'I'm not like that!'

'You haven't reported the Mondeo as missing so you'll probably lose out on the insurance' said Adrian. 'It was worth about three, maybe four grand? That'll be a lot out of your pocket money when Daddy gets home'.

Liam began rocking on the chair again.

'Liam, we can tell you're bursting to say something to us' said Ollie. 'So come on, out with it. We can keep you here for hours if necessary until you talk'.

'He was a mate of my Dad's, alright?'

'Who was?'

'The guy who took the Mondeo' Liam explained. 'He's been a mate of my Dad's for years, they go way back'.

'So it wasn't Leo McKenzie who took the car?'

'No' said Liam. 'But Leo organized it all on behalf of this other bloke'.

'Why did he do that?'

'I don't know, I just don't know. All I do know is that a whole group of them get together to pick up young girls. My Dad offered to include me but I said I didn't want any part in it. I thought it was disgusting. I thought my Dad was disgusting and I still do'.

Ollie glanced fleetingly at the solicitor who'd gone as white as a sheet. 'Your Dad is on holiday in Florida, Liam'.

'Yeah I know but he left instructions before he left'.

' Do you realise what you've just implicated your father in, Liam?'

'Yes' said Liam, looking down and ashamed. 'But somebody's got to stop them'.

'What was the name of this other bloke you keep talking about, Liam?' Adrian questioned.

'I don't know' Liam answered. 'I just know he was something to do with Leo McKenzie'.

When they went down to arrest Leo McKenzie Jeff and DI Rebecca Stockton were communicating in that very professional way of clipped voices and avoiding any lapses into conversations about personal matters. Just stick to the job is what they were saying to each other without saying anything at all.

They arrested McKenzie at the school he taught at just off the Ashton New Road. They kind of thought he may not come quietly but he protested rather more loudly than they'd expected. It must have been a reaction to the embarrassment they'd caused him by arresting him at the school in front of all the students and staff. Well they didn't use stocks anymore to humiliate apprehended law breakers but this was the modern equivalent and just as effective.

They brought him to the station where a DNA sample was taken. Then they put him in a cell and made him sweat for a while.

TWELVE

DC Joe Alexander had been inwardly basking in his newly emerging relationship with DI Rebecca Stockton. It had been a long time since he'd felt anything like this and they'd spent every night together for the last week. And much as they were telling each other that it was all meant to be very casual with no strings and no promises and no talk of the future, it was clear that something was happening between them that amounted to something that was much more than a friends with benefits type of situation. But whatever it was it was providing him with a great sense of well being.

In the meantime there was an investigation to be dealt with and Joe was nothing if not a diligent police officer who liked nothing more than to link clues together to make a case against a criminal or group of criminals. And this was how the picture was emerging as he sat at his computer and went through everything of any potential significance that could get them to nail someone for the murder of Sheridan Taylor.

He was about to make a call to check some details with regard to Leo McKenzie's employment record when one of the uniformed officers came upstairs and told him there was a woman waiting in reception who wanted to speak to the officers in charge of the investigation into the murder of Sheridan Taylor. Joe was the only one there at the time. DSI Barton and Rebecca had been back briefly but then went out again almost straight away when they received a call from a Jeanette Adams to say that her daughter Hayley was missing and had gone to the same school as Sheridan Taylor and was taught by Leo McKenzie who she'd just heard had been arrested. So Joe put on his jacket, straightened his tie and went downstairs. The woman was waiting in one of the interview rooms just off the reception area.

'Hello?' said Joe. 'I'm DC Joe Alexander. I understand you may have some information regarding the murder of Sheridan Taylor? Please sit down'

'Thank you. I'm Catherine McKenzie and you're holding my son Leo here'.

Joe immediately pricked up his ears. This could end up being dynamite. She was a smart woman who Joe perceived to be in about her mid to late fifties and the dark blue of her two piece jacket and skirt contrasted with the white of her blouse. It looked like she'd come straight from work. Joe sometimes wished he didn't make instant mental appraisals of people he'd just met. But then he wouldn't be a very effective police officer. In fact he wouldn't be a police officer. He'd just be a nosey bastard.

'Yes we are holding your son' Joe confirmed. 'But how can we help you?'

'Officer, I brought my son up alone. I never had another relationship with a man after Leo's father. My brother and my father have both provided male role models in his life but he's never seen me with another man. I took the decision that I would devote myself entirely to Leo whilst he grew up and now I've probably missed the boat forever'.

Joe felt an overwhelming sadness for this woman who certainly hadn't lost her looks but who'd shut herself off from a romantic life to raise a son who looks like he may have turned out so terribly wrong. There must be a part of her that regrets making such a massive mistake. She's thrown her life away.

'Did Leo ever meet his father?'

'No' said Catherine. 'His father was never interested but I think it'll turn out to be highly relevant to your investigation if I tell you about him'.

'Then please do'.

'Frank and I went out together for about a year. This was back in the early eighties and I was besotted with him. We had what the young ones would call today a wild time. But then he suddenly started to lose interest in me sexually. I was pregnant with Leo by this time although I didn't yet know it but Frank started spending more and more time away from me. It was hard because we'd become so close but looking back I think he was using me'.

'In what way?'

'To try and feel normal' said Catherine. She looked down and hesitated for a moment. 'I found a stash of magazines. Don't forget we didn't have the internet back then and it sounds very old fashioned now but I looked at these magazines and I threw up. They were devoted to men who are into having sex with underage girls'.

'That can't have been easy to say the least'.

'You're right it wasn't. I was absolutely horrified. In the meantime I discovered that I was pregnant and I confronted Frank. There was a case at the time concerning the disappearance of seven underage girls in our area of Hyde. The case was never solved. It wasn't all that long since the moors murderers and people in this part of the world were still jumpy about children disappearing because of Brady and Hindley. We had the most flaming row but during it Frank admitted that he and his so-called friends had been behind the disappearance of the girls. This was probably one of the first cases of what we now call grooming in this country. And these were all white men including John Nightingale who owns Farndale motors in Littleborough. I've known John a long time and he knows I know what he's always got up to'.

That name certainly rang a bell with Joe as being part of the investigation and his eyes were opening wider with each revelation Catherine McKenzie made. 'So you're saying that Leo's father Frank was a member of a grooming gang back in the early eighties? But why is that relevant to us now?'

'Because he carried on' said Catherine. 'I've brought you a file giving you details of this sort of thing happening in different parts of the northwest at regular intervals since that case in nineteen eighty-three. I've regularly checked the crime records for this particular kind of crime for the last thirty years and that's how I've managed to put my file together. Now I know that Frank has been in touch with Leo recently. I've seen text messages on his mobile. I'm sorry to say that Frank may have swept up his own son in his vile, sickening behaviour'.

'Miss McKenzie, why did you collect these crime details for your file? And have you ever reported any of your suspicions to the police?'

'The answer to your second question is no. The answer to your first question is that I was hoping to be able to hand it over to the police one day'.

'I don't understand? What stopped you before?'

Catherine took a deep breath. 'Someone has been protecting Frank and the rest of the gang for the last thirty years'.

'You believe it was someone in the police?'

'The gang have never been prosecuted, never been investigated, and none of them have any criminal record. How could that have happened for all these years if there wasn't someone protecting them? We know it can happen, officer'.

'But how do you know it's happened with this gang?'

'Because I went to the police with my initial findings thirty years ago' said Catherine. 'I was threatened. I was told to go away and keep quiet or else. I was pregnant and alone. I didn't have much choice but to do what they told me to. But now Frank has involved his own son I have to try again to see if someone can do something to stop them once and for all. Also

I could be rather ill, you see? My doctor thinks I may have cancer. I'd like to see justice for all these girls before it's too late for me'.

'Leo, a lot of new information has come to light with regard to your relationship with Frank Leadbetter' said Jeff as he and DI Rebecca Stockton began their interview of Leo.

'You've already kept my client waiting here for an intolerably long time, detective' said Marcus Dewsbury the duty solicitor. 'It's time you got to the point of why you've brought him here'.

'And we will, Mr. Dewsbury' said Jeff. 'But the new information we have is very pertinent to our investigation and possible case against your client. So bear with us please'. He turned to Leo. 'Leo, who contacted who? Was it you or was it your father Frank Leadbetter?'

'I always said I'd never try and find my father' said Leo. 'A lot of my friends had urged me to but out of respect for my mother I never tried. I thought it might embarrass her because I knew something terrible must've happened or otherwise why wouldn't she ever talk to me about him? I thought that if it didn't embarrass her then it would probably hurt her and I'd feel like I'd slapped her in the face and been very disloyal'.

'So do I take it your father contacted you?' said Jeff who was watching Leo McKenzie as he went over every word. His earlier bravado at the school had been replaced by a solemn kind of sulkiness. At the school when they arrested him he didn't know his mother was talking to them at the same time and probably didn't know much else about what she told them.

'About six months ago I got a call from him just out of the blue' said Leo. 'He said he'd seen me in the paper when I got an award for being a good teacher. I've never asked him how he got my number so I can't tell you that. All I do know is that I was as pleased as punch to hear from him even after all these years'.

'What was your first meeting like?'

'It was in a pub in the city centre' Leo revealed. 'I immediately recognized him because we are very alike. You can tell we're father and son and after thirty years of not knowing him I kind of really got off on that, you know?'

'Yeah, that's understandable. Go on?'

'We went out drinking a couple of times and in that short time we became very close' said Leo. He reached out for a glass of water that was sitting on the table. His hand was shaking. 'He introduced me to the … '

' … to the what, Leo? He introduced you to the pleasures of what?'

'Of … of pre-pubescent teenage flesh' Leo stammered. His eyes were filling up. 'I'd always secretly been into underage teenage girls but I'd never acted on it, I swear I'd never acted on it until my father urged me to'.

'And did you start with Sheridan Taylor?'

Leo nodded his head. 'Yes. I had a thing for her right from when she joined our school. I knew she was unhappy at home and I knew she was vulnerable. She seemed to like me and one night I went for it. I made my move'.

'Where was this?'

'At my father's flat in Alexandra Park. That's where I took her'.

'We'll need the address, Leo'.

'Oh I can give you that and I can give you a picture of my father too. That's not a problem'.

DI Rebecca Stockton was having a problem listening to all this. The filthy bastard had just admitted to liking underage girls like someone would express a liking for anything that was innocent. Except this wasn't innocent. This was about using children for the sexual gratification of adults. This was sick.

'Did you know she was pregnant, Leo?'

'No' said Leo. His tears started falling down his cheeks. 'No, I didn't, I swear I didn't'.

'What happened last Sunday afternoon, Leo?'

'My father said that the pleasures we were now both fond of should be shared' Leo explained. 'He said he wanted Sheridan'.

'And you agreed just like that?'

'I thought it was a way of … well a way of keeping him close, keeping him with me after being without him all those years'.

'Even though you knew fine and well what he was like?'

'I guess he had some kind of hold on me' said Leo who then wiped his mouth with the back of his hand. It's what happens when your father comes into your life after thirty-two years. You fall under a kind of spell. 'Anyway, we followed her to the petrol station but then I couldn't handle it anymore. I got out the car and legged it'.

'You left Sheridan to your father's mercy?'

'It's not like she didn't know him. She'd met him on several occasions'.

'Oh so that makes it alright then' said Leo. 'If a girl knows the man it's alright for him to rape her in the back of his car and then set fire to it. How do you think she felt, Leo? How do you think she felt in those final few moments of life after she'd been raped by your father and was then about to burn to death?'

'I don't know!' Leo cried. 'I don't know! I'm sorry'.

'Sorry? It's a bit late for that, Leo. You see, we've received a report of another young girl who's been found dead in the bedroom of a house in Moston. Thirteen years old. Remind you of anyone? Perhaps you'd like to come with us when we go and tell her mother? She'd been sexually assaulted repeatedly and had been plied with so much alcohol that she ended up choking on her own vomit. I repeat, Leo, she was thirteen years old. Her name was Hayley Adams and she was in your class at school. Did you introduce her to your father, Leo? Is that how it worked? Is that how the process started that meant she ended up dying in what must've been the most terrifying of circumstances?'

Leo cried again. 'Yes! Yes, that's what happened. And I'm sorry. I can't say anymore than that. I'm just really, really sorry'.

'What made you confess now, Leo? What made you come clean as much as a man like you can come clean?'

'I sent my father a text when I saw you driving up to the school' said Leo. 'I knew you were coming for me. I asked him what I should do and he texted me back with four short words'.

'Which were?'

'You're on your own'.

'I see' said Jeff. 'So he left you out there on a limb'.

Leo started to cry again. 'And that's when it hit me. All those years I had with Mum who brought me up, loved me, cared for me, did everything she could for me, made sure I did something with my life and became a teacher. All those years and then five minutes with my father and he turned me into a pervert. I'm sorry Sheridan killed that bloke and I'm so, so sorry for the way she died. I didn't know she was carrying our baby, I swear I didn't. And I'm sorry for Hayley who I know was so unhappy'.

Jeff sat back in his chair. The job was almost done.

'Leo, we'll be typing up a statement for you to sign and then charging you'.

'Well it's no good going after my father' said Leo. 'He was always saying that he'd never go down for anything'.

'How could he be so sure?'

'I don't know'.

THIRTEEN

'It all fits, Sir' said DS Ollie Wright after he'd helped DC Joe Alexander take the relevant facts from the file that Catherine McKenzie had given him and put them all together for the DSI who'd just come up from charging Leo McKenzie. 'The disappearance of young teenage underage girls having certainly been groomed across several cities in the northwest during the past thirty years. Some were as young as ten. Some have never been found but those that were have normally been in the same state as little Hayley Adams'.

'The house in Moston where Hayley was found was full of empty coke and lemonade bottles plus empty bottles of vodka, gin, and Bacardi, Sir' Joe added. 'The press cuttings that Catherine McKenzie has collected down the years are all of similar scenes'.

'How does it add up in terms of how many girls disappeared in this way over the years?' asked DC Adrian Bradshaw.

'Almost a hundred' Ollie revealed.

'What?' asked Jeff incredulously.

'It's true, Sir' said Ollie. 'And there's nothing on the system to say that any enquiries have been carried out by the Greater Manchester force or any other in the region. It's as if the various police forces collectively turned their backs on it all, Sir'.

'But why for God's sake?' Adrian pressed.

'And how can that be?' asked DI Rebecca Stockton who was having none of this. She stepped on the line every second of every working day and she had no time for those of her colleagues who weren't as strong or as diligent about the rules that they all had to abide by if they were to have any credibility as police officers. Especially when she was facing an official enquiry for taking a calculated risk that may or may not have paid off whilst others may be getting away with turning their back on the grooming of underage girls leading to murder. 'Alright, thirty years ago I can imagine from what I know about what went on back in those days that it could've happened. But over the years we've tightened up so much on internal corruption. And I just can't get my head around it happening today on this scale. I just can't'.

'But these are the ones we know about' said DC Adrian Bradshaw. 'I don't like to think of it but there's probably hundreds more'.

This was one of those occasions when Jeff really wished he didn't know what he was beginning to find out. He'd already busted a senior officer for corruption a few years back and it had taken him a while to live that down amongst some of his colleagues. But this was completely on another level and he knew he had to do something about it.

'DSI Barton?'

They all looked up at the sound of Chief Superintendent Chambers' voice and she stood in the doorway.

'DSI Barton, could I speak to you in my office, please?'

Taking the file with him Jeff followed the Chief Super to her office where she asked him to close the door behind them and take a seat. She gestured to the two armchairs in the window. Jeff wondered what this was all about but had a sneaking suspicion that it was something to do with the file in his hands.

'I see you've made an arrest' said Chambers.

'Yes, ma'am. Leo McKenzie. He's a bit of a sad case but that doesn't make any difference when you break the law'.

'Good, well leave it there, Jeff'.

'Sorry?'

'I don't want any more arrests to be made in connection with this investigation'.

Jeff could feel the anger rising in him. 'Ma'am, the body of a thirteen year-old girl, Hayley Adams, has been found in a house where she'd been sexually assaulted repeatedly and plied with alcohol which she eventually choked on. Are you really saying to me that I have to piss this investigation down the drain?'

'Can you please choose your words a little more delicately, DSI Barton'.

Jeff had always found it curious when people object to you using swear words and yet have no problem listening to the evil things human beings do to each other. He found it so bloody hypocritical and so very bloody British.

'Can you at least tell me why, ma'am?'

'I'm not at liberty to do that, no'.

'So what am I going to tell my team who've been working all the hours God sends to crack this case?'

'That there's insufficient evidence to support taking the investigation any further and with resources being stretched you've decided to wrap things up'.

'Oh no, no, no' said Jeff. 'I'm not taking the flak for this. They will be outraged'.

'Then tell them what you like, Jeff, but this investigation stops here and now'.

'So what do I do about Leo McKenzie's father, Frank Leadbetter who Leo has given me more than enough evidence to bring him in on?'

'I said it stops here and now, Jeff'.

'And what about justice for Hayley Adams and indeed for Sheridan Taylor?'

'I'm not going to keep on repeating myself, Jeff'.

'No wonder you wouldn't give us any extra resources' said Jeff. 'What's behind all this, ma'am?'

'What do you mean?'

'We are law enforcement' Jeff emphasized. 'We uphold the law and bring the guilty to face justice. We don't ignore it and let the guilty go free'.

'For once DSI Barton I'm asking you to heed my orders without your usual questioning!'

Jeff was absolutely seething. He went back to the team and told them the bad news. Then they were all seething too but he emphasized the need for them all to go home, lick their wounds and come back in the morning to face a new challenge and a new day.

'That was a load of old bullshit' said Rebecca after the other three had gone and she decided to stay behind for a bit of a chat with the boss.

'Aren't you going off with Joe?'

'I said I'd catch him up in half an hour' said Rebecca. 'They've all gone to the pub'.

Jeff took out the bottle of scotch and two glasses he kept in one of his drawers and poured out a measure in each. He handed one to Rebecca.

'It can't end here, Jeff'.

'It has to, Becky'.

'But for fuck's sake, Jeff! We can't ignore this. We can't let Frank Leadbetter walk away with being a possible multi-murderer. Not to mention John Nightingale and the countless others'.

'Well we've got to because we've got no choice!' Jeff repeated, firmly.

'He said he'd get away with it no matter what he did' said Rebecca. 'So someone has to be protecting him'.

'Yes I had worked that out, Becky'.

'Someone who needs exposing'.

'Yep, I'd got to that one too'.

'Then there's got to be something we can do' Rebecca pleaded.

'Not that I can see for the moment, Becky. Maybe we'll find something but not as it stands now. Chambers made her position crystal bloody clear'.

Rebecca then had an idea but she didn't want to run it by Jeff in case he expressly forbade her to even think about it. So instead she supped up the rest of her scotch and put her glass down on Jeff's desk.

'Are you coming over to the pub?'

'No' said Jeff. 'I'm going to go home to my son'.

Rebecca smiled. 'I thought that would be your answer'.

'I know I'm a sad bastard who won't get off his arse and get a life and when he does finally decide to he finds he's too late'.

Rebecca blushed. 'I didn't mean that'.

'No, I know you didn't. Now get off to the pub and I'll see you in the morning'.

After Rebecca left Jeff sat back and closed his eyes for a moment. He daydreamed about his late wife Lillie Mae and wished he could reach out and touch her. Then he was brought back to real life by the phone ringing on his desk.

'DSI Barton?'

'Oh hello, is that DSI Jeff Barton?'

The voice was that of a woman. A confident sounding woman. 'Yes, that's me. Who am I talking to?'

'I'm Martha Langton. I'm the Labour party's shadow home secretary?'

Jeff suddenly sat up. 'Oh yes, look, of course, I'm sorry. I had a note to say you'd called when I came back from leave. I should've called you back'.

'Oh no that's okay' said Martha who liked the sound of this police officer's voice. Well, she may be happily married but that doesn't mean she's dead. 'Can I call you Jeff?'

'Of course you can' said Jeff.

'Great. And I'm Martha. 'The thing is, Jeff, I've got some information and I think you're the person I should share it with'.

'Information about what?'

'I don't really want to talk about it on the phone' said Martha who'd been checking up and found out what Jeff was working on. It gave her the perfect way in. 'But as a matter of fact it has to do with the case you're dealing with at the moment'.

'Yes?'

'Well I think I have some information you need to know' said Martha. 'But can I ask you not to tell anyone that we're going to meet? The reason will be clear once I've shared the information with you'.

'Well yes that's fine' said Jeff. 'When and where?'

'How about tomorrow morning at my constituency office on Palatine Road? Say about ten?'

'Okay, that's fine'.

'Thanks, Jeff. I'll see you in the morning'.

The following morning Jeff made his way to Martha's constituency office for ten o'clock. It wasn't hard to find once he got to the right end of Palatine Road. There were pictures of her plastered all over the windows. He'd better not tell her he voted Liberal Democrat at the last election and was thinking of voting Green at the upcoming one.

Jeff was shown into Martha's private office where he was more than pleasantly surprised by his host. She had the most beguiling of big blue eyes that the television cameras really didn't do justice to. He knew she was a forthright politician. He knew that she'd exposed a paedophile ring that had claimed many innocent victims and that she didn't seem to care who she upset on the way to standing up for a cause. He'd admired her from afar and agreed with much of what she'd said in her capacity as the Labour shadow home secretary. He hadn't expected to see her as a woman who he could actually fancy.

'I'm sorry for all the cloak and dagger stuff' said Martha from behind her desk. Jeff was sitting in front of it with a mug of coffee that her staff had made for him. 'And how's your coffee?'

Jeff's coffee tasted absolutely disgusting. It was so bloody weak. 'It's great, thank you. Now how can I help you?'

Martha described how she'd had a document placed under the door of her Westminster office which had led to her exposure of a paedophile ring earlier in the year. She then showed him the remainder of the document. The bit she hadn't been able to show anyone so far because it was so explosive. But it also corresponded with what Jeff had found out in the course of the investigation and it was that connection that lit the fire in Jeff's interest.

'This says that a group of individuals have been allowed to get away with grooming underage teenage girls as a way of reducing the underclass of the uneducated who would never contribute anything positively to society' said Jeff in complete disbelief of what the words were telling him.

'That's it' said Martha.

'But this is absolutely disgraceful' said Jeff. 'How on earth has this been allowed to carry on?'

'Precisely because someone and it still doesn't name who, but some establishment figure somewhere has been controlling it all. Whoever that is has been using these pathetic excuses for men and their proclivity for underage girls to reduce the numbers of the underclass. It's kind of another form of ethnic cleansing. It's certainly fascist and evil. And it has to be stopped'.

'Our investigation has been brought to a close, you know?'

'That doesn't surprise me' said Martha who was liking Jeff more as their conversation went on. He was one of those new style of sensitive coppers that she so liked to deal with.

'But it was an order from my Chief Superintendent'.

'Yes but it wouldn't have been their decision. It would've come from way higher up'.

'So what can be done?'

'Jeff, I've got an idea but it requires a big ask of you'.

Jeff smiled. 'Why did you choose to approach me anyway?'

'Because of the way you handled the child murder case last year' Martha explained. 'The poor lad who was murdered lived in my constituency which means that you do too. I could only observe from afar, but it seemed like you dealt with the matter in an intelligent sane way'.

'That's part of the job, Martha'.

'I know but you looked like the sort of officer I could do business with as the old saying goes'.

'Well I'm flattered' said Jeff. It was always good when somebody noticed what you did. 'But tell me more about this idea of yours?'

'I'll need to see the file you've collected on this recent investigation into Sheridan Taylor and Hayley Adams. I'll need the names of the people you've been prevented from apprehending'.

'Aren't you taking something of a risk? I mean, if this hasn't been exposed before it's for a very good reason to do with their security and the information you received was in an anonymous document which means that whoever passed it on didn't want to be known. Martha, you're dealing with establishment figures that operate in a realm far beyond the world of the ordinary copper like me'.

'And that's precisely why I need to stop them, Jeff' Martha emphasized. 'Don't you see? That's the whole point of this'.

They talked on for another half an hour although not just about what Martha's intentions were. They talked about the home office and its relationship with the police, about the police and the way they worked. They also talked about family, children, Jeff losing Lillie Mae. They knew a lot about each other after that conversation.

'I'm asking you to take a risk too, Jeff' said Martha. 'I mean I won't name you or any of your squad but your bosses are bound to put two and two together as to where I got my information'.

Jeff smiled. 'Yes, well if we're right and this thing is smashed then nobody will bother anymore'.

SB FOURTEEN

DI Rebecca Stockton still hadn't calmed down from the team having had the rug pulled from underneath them. She didn't blame Jeff. He was just following orders that couldn't be challenged but Rebecca had thought about another way around the problem of getting to the guilty like Frank Leadbetter and John Nightingale. Having Leo McKenzie in custody meant something but it was like when they caught the small time drug dealers. It didn't make a scrap of difference to the drugs trade around the city. Only catching the men at the top would do that.

She pulled up outside the address they had for Frank Leadbetter in Alexandra Park. She looked up at the small two storey block of flats with its well kept gardens and tidy hedges. A very acceptable place to live, she thought. Too bloody good for the likes of this evil bastard.

She got out of her car and walked round to the back of the block. It was fairly quiet at this time of the morning. All the folks who worked had gone already and it was lull period between the rush hour and the business of the day getting going.

Her intention was to take Frank Leadbetter in and force the issue with whoever was trying to protect him. On the way she'd be informing the press so that the job of whoever was protecting him would be made that much harder. She didn't care about what her superiors thought of her for doing it. Some of them must be part of the problem.

An outside staircase led up to number four. Yes, this would make her a maverick but so fucking be it. She hadn't told Joe what she was planning to do. They were all supposed to be on a day off to make up for some of the hours they'd lost during the course of the investigation. She'd left him asleep in bed and she'd take him some lunch back later. Bless him. He was a good man.

She hadn't told Jeff about her plans either. She did feel a bit guilty about that. It would embarrass him with Chambers and the like but in the grand scheme of what she was trying to do here did that really matter?

She rang the doorbell but there was no answer so she tried the door handle and to her great surprise it was open. She let herself in and called out 'Frank Leadbetter? This is the police, are you in there?'

The door opened straight onto the lounge with its light brown carpet and dark brown suite. Directly opposite was a door to a hallway and what looked like the kitchen beyond. A tall, head shaved man in a black tracksuit came into the room.

'Are you Frank Leadbetter'

'For the last fifty-seven years, yes. Who are you?'

'I'm detective inspector Rebecca Stockton, Greater Manchester police' said Rebecca and held up her warrant card.

'Congratulations'.

Rebecca couldn't get over how so fucking casual he was being. Standing there as if nothing in the world mattered and nobody could touch him. And that smirk on his face. Urgh!

'I'd like you to accompany me to the station, Mr. Leadbetter'.

'You're far too old for me, darling. Do you get my meaning?'

Rebecca was disgusted as if she'd been wrapped in his filth. 'Mr. Leadbetter we need to speak to you about the murder of Sheridan Taylor, Hayley Adams, and several other cases dating back thirty years. Now are you going to come quietly or am I going to have to arrest you?'

'Handcuffs? I like a bit of that'.

'Is that one of the compliance measures you used on your victims?'

'Darling, I'm not coming down to the station with you or to any other fucking place' Leadbetter sneered. 'Now get to fuck. I've got things to do'.

'Right' said Rebecca. 'Frank Leadbetter, I'm arresting you for the murder of … '

' … you're wasting your breath, officer'.

The second man's voice came from behind her and Rebecca turned to see a tall suntanned man in about his mid to late forties with a full head of black hair. He had nothing on his feet and was dressed only in a t-shirt and a pair of shorts. He'd clearly just got out of bed.

And he was holding a gun that was pointed right at her.

'Put the gun down, sir' said Rebecca. She'd only faced a gunman once before in her career and that time it had scared her out of her wits too.

'Allow me to introduce myself' said the man. 'I'm Brian Taylor. I'm Sheridan's father'.

Frank was as shocked to hear the news as Rebecca. 'Brian Taylor? You told me your name was Cliff. You said you wanted a piece of the action and that you knew me through my associates in Spain. You've double fucking crossed me'.

'That's right' said Taylor. 'And it feels good to see you looking scared. It must be what my little girl looked like before you burned her alive'.

Frank grabbed Rebecca and held her in front of him.

'Hiding behind a woman police officer' Taylor snarled. 'How fucking low can you get? I did a lot to hurt my family and now I'm going to put it right'.

'Mr. Taylor, please put the gun down, this is not the way to sort this' Rebecca pleaded.

'I don't want him living and breathing in jail even if you could make charges stick against him' said Taylor. 'I want him to burn in the fires of Hell. It's an eye for an eye, Leadbetter. You murdered my little girl and now I've come for you'.

'I let you into my home' said Leadbetter. 'I didn't even know you had a gun'.

'You really are the most useless fucker' said Taylor. 'All you've done all your life is rape little girls'.

'Mr. Taylor, I'm asking you again to please put the gun down' Rebecca pleaded once more.

'How did you know it was me?' Leadbetter demanded.

'Your associates, as you like to call them, in Spain speak freely when you offer them enough Euros and speak to the right ones'.

'The duplicitous bastards'.

'Yeah, that's a phrase I'd use. But it's better to be a duplicitous bastard than someone who rapes and murders little girls'.

Rebecca suddenly felt the full force of Leadbetter's strength as he pushed her towards Taylor and then made a dash for the door. Leadbetter heard the gun go off but didn't turn to look. He was halfway down the stairs when he felt the first bullet in his back. The second one went into his head and he felt no more in this world. He slumped forward at the bottom of the stairs into a pool of his own blood.

Taylor sat on the stairs, completely out of breath. He was satisfied that he'd got Leadbetter and revenge for poor Sheridan. He was only sorry that in the heat of the moment he'd shot and killed an innocent police woman.

Martha Langton made her statement to one of the last sessions of the House of Commons before parliament was dissolved ahead of the upcoming general election. She outlined everything in Catherine McKenzie's file and how it all pointed to a group of men whose crimes against underage teenage girls who they groomed for sex and then for murder and were being protected by someone in the British establishment who thought of it as a good way of culling the underclass of Britain. She boldly and shamelessly named names from Frank Leadbetter and John Nightingale all the way through every name Catherine had managed to gather.

'Mr. deputy speaker, this kind of shadowy action by faceless members of the British establishment cannot be tolerated in our modern democracy. It harks back to an era when people at the bottom of the social scale had no rights and their lives didn't matter. It leads to men like Brian Taylor taking the law into their own hands and an innocent police woman, DI Rebecca Stockton, losing her life when she tried to smash the system of injustice. Well I for one will not tolerate this any longer. I demand that the government initiate an enquiry, and I mean before the general election, into how these crimes went unsolved for so long and I'll be happy to share my information with that enquiry. We owe it to all those girls who lost their lives without anyone taking account of it'.

In the pub after Rebecca's funeral Jeff took his pint and went over and sat next to a very forlorn looking Joe Alexander.

'It's tough, isn't it?' said Jeff.

'You could say that, Sir'.

'I think you can call me Jeff here, Joe'.

'You had feelings for her too, didn't you, Jeff?'

'Yes I did but they were complicated' Jeff admitted. 'If we'd met at a different time or place … perhaps something might have worked properly between us. I don't know, Joe. It's always easy to be wise after the event'.

'Do you worry about whether or not you're ever going to be happy again?'

'I do sometimes' said Jeff. 'What about you?

'Well without sounding too dramatic it just seems that whenever I get a taste of happiness it gets snatched away from me after such a short time. I can't find anything that lasts. Rebecca and me had only just got started, you know?'

'Joe, mate, I can't say it will all work out for you one day because I don't know and I have a bit of an uncomfortable relationship with the idea of hope. It comes from being made a widower when you're barely into your thirties. But I will say this. It can happen to others so why can't it happen to you?'

'I thought it had happened' said Joe. 'That's the point'.

Joe felt like he was getting a bit lost in his own grief. He couldn't imagine what it would be like to lose your wife and be left to bring up a kid by yourself. But then again he couldn't imagine what it's like to have a wife so he decided to change the subject.

'I see that Martha Langton seems like she'd done well' said Joe. 'Scores of arrests have been made. Their protection must've abandoned them'.

'It would seem so and yes, I think Martha Langton has done extremely well'.

Chief Superintendent Chambers came over and said she was leaving. She asked Jeff if she could speak to him in the car park.

'This must bring back a lot of unhappy memories for you, Jeff' she said once they'd reached her car.

'Yes, ma'am. It's not been the easiest of days'.

'You've shown great strength, Jeff, throughout all this awful business with Rebecca. It says a lot about you'.

'Well she was a very gifted officer and a close friend, ma'am. But I'll be glad when I wake up tomorrow and it's another day'.

'We'll need to find a replacement for her'.

'Are you sure you've got the resources, ma'am?'

Chambers smiled. 'Very droll, Jeff. We could of course promote from within to the new DI position and recruit another DC?'

'I think Ollie Wright would be perfect as the new DI of the team, ma'am'.

'And I agree' said Chambers. 'We'll work on that basis then. And by the way, the shadow home secretary has done a very good job with the information that was passed to her and which has now formed part of a major operation. You don't know how she got that information, do you?'

'I believe it was anonymously passed under her Westminster office door, ma'am'.

'Jeff, I mean the meaty stuff that allowed her to move forward'.

Jeff looked down at the ground and said 'Information passes through all sorts of channels, ma'am'.

'And that's your answer?'

'I don't have another one'.

Chambers smiled again. 'Whoever did pass that information to Martha Langton was of course, on reflection, doing exactly the right thing even if some feathers within our own force have been ruffled'.

'Then I hope they're pleased with themselves, ma'am'.

'So do I because they deserve to be'.

'I agree, ma'am'.

'I'll see you in the morning, Jeff'.

Jeff drove home wondering about life and how he was going to cope with the loss of a second woman from it. But he did console himself with the knowledge that so many perverts were now being rounded up and charges were being made against them. At least that could be taken from all this mess even though he wished to God Rebecca had told him what she was intending to do so he could've stopped her.

His sister Annabel and her son Kyle who live in a flat just down the road from him were coming round for dinner tonight. His brother Lewis and his partner Seamus were also coming. His live in Nanny and housekeeper Brendan would be cooking it all and he'd sit down with them to eat too seeing as he was considered part of the family. It was going to be a lovely evening with his nearest and dearest during which he'd remember Rebecca and the life that perhaps they could've had.

He pulled up onto his drive and saw his little son Toby waving at him through the window. It made his heart leap. Life had taken a lot from him but it had also given him so much.

THE END

But DSI Jeff Barton will be back in 'THROWN DOWN' later in 2015.

Meanwhile, have you tried his series featuring Sydney-based private investigator 'Stephanie Marshall?' The latest is called 'COULD MAX BURLEY BE A KILLER?' and on the next page you can take a sneak preview of the first chapter.

In the line of business Stephanie Marshall was in she was used to having uncomfortable experiences. It went with the job that some of the people she came across weren't exactly the full quid. She'd recently had a case where a woman had asked her to follow her boyfriend because she suspected he was up to no good with another woman. A run of the mill sort of case at face value and Stephanie spent several days keeping the boyfriend under surveillance and taking pictures of his activities. But she didn't see him with any other woman in a situation that suggested he may be playing away from home and when she broached her findings with her client the client broke down and started sobbing in Stephanie's arms. The 'deliriously happy couple with no issues' had been on one date five months ago after which the 'boyfriend' decided that he didn't want to take things any further. But the 'girlfriend' had been so desperate to be with someone that she'd deluded herself into believing the date had been one of the happiest nights of her life and a wonderful relationship had ensued, even to the extent of believing he was two timing her and employing Stephanie's services to find out. She'd built up a whole relationship with this man but only in her head. Stephanie did some more probing and found that her client, who was in her early forties, had never been married and hadn't even had a boyfriend for several years. She had a reputation where she worked for being a particularly bitter and twisted woman who delighted in 'reporting' her colleagues to management for the slightest of misdemeanors and who was always critical of other people's relationships especially if the girl was young and pretty. Stephanie sympathized with the sad psycho bitch but arranged for her to see a therapist who could perhaps help her to sort out her real 'issues'.

Then there was the farmer from the Northern Territories who asked Stephanie if she could find out where his seventeen year-old daughter was because she'd run away from home and he believed she was in Sydney. She'd felt quite sorry for him at first. He'd looked completely lost and woebegone in the big city and he explained that there'd been a huge family argument after which his daughter had shot through. Stephanie did manage to find the man's daughter but the situation she learned about wasn't quite as the father had explained. She told Stephanie that her father had been steadily losing it in his head and had been hitting out at her with his fists especially when he came home drunk from the pub and she hadn't been able to stand it any longer. But Stephanie had managed to get father and daughter talking again and the father agreed to seek help. He said that the reason for him cracking up was because his farm was going bankrupt and he didn't know what to do. Stephanie learned the extent of his cash problems when she presented him with her bill and he tried to pay her in live pythons, three of them to be precise, all in a large tank on the back of his truck that he'd driven all the way down from just outside Darwin. 'Bloody valuable these big bastards, sweetheart' he'd pointed out. 'You'll be able to sell them to any zoo or if you want to make serious money then sell them to some scientific sort of place who'll use them for experiments'. Stephanie said she'd prefer to keep his account open until he was able to pay her in straightforward cash and he could return the snakes to the outback where they belonged.

But lately Stephanie had been presented with potentially one of her most challenging clients. She hadn't spoken to him but as she looked out of her office window she saw him standing across the road and looking up at her office like he'd done every day for the past week. She recognized him. She knew just who he was. His face had been splashed across the newspapers and the TV news channels and although the average man or woman hadn't committed his physique to memory, professionals like Stephanie took a deeper interest than others would. He obviously wanted to employ her services but it was becoming exasperating because every time she went downstairs and out onto the street to try and talk to him he disappeared. It was as if he was reaching out for help but couldn't quite go through with it. He must be in a worse way than the media would have everyone believe. After all everybody thinks he's a cold blooded killer.

She turned from the window and tried to focus on her email inbox which currently totalled 152. She scrolled down the list and came to the one that really mattered. It was from her eldest son James back in the UK who was coming down to stay in a couple of weeks time and spend his gap year with her before starting university. The email contained details of his flight into Sydney and she noted it down with great excitement. She hadn't seen either of her two sons James and Matthew since she went back to the UK last Christmas and was so looking forward to having at least one of her boys in her arms again. She still called them her boys even though they were both very tall young men.

She'd just finished her reply to James when the buzzer for her office went off and the security camera showed that it was the man who'd been looking up at her window. She pressed to let him into the building and a few minutes later she heard his footsteps coming up the stairs to the second floor and then she saw the shape of him in a shadow against the frosted glass of her office door. She'd been meaning to get the frosted glass replaced because not only was it a bit of a cliche for a private investigator but it quite often spooked her out when an image appeared. She pressed the button to unlock the door and he came in.

'Hello?' he said, holding out his hand though more out of manners than confidence. 'My name is Max Burley'.

'Yes' said Stephanie who stood up and shook his hand. 'I recognise you'.

'I thought you might'.

'Please sit down' said Stephanie who was immediately struck by Burley. The pictures of him in the papers and on TV didn't do justice to the man in his late thirties who was one of the most handsome men she'd ever come across. Leaving her darling Peter out of it who in any case was more rugged than handsome, Max Burley had the most perfect dark brown eyes in a flawless face with a wide mouth and no visible lines. He also had that strong outdoor look of one of those naturalists you see on TV chasing wildlife all over the place. He must spend a lot of his time outside. He had large upper arm and shoulder muscles and was dressed in a pair of dark blue jeans, maroon t-shirt under a black leather bomber jacket with a zip fastener. His dark brown hair was short but there was turmoil written right across that face. He looked brooding, like he just didn't know what to do. 'So why has it taken you all this time to actually come and talk to me?'

'I was nervous' said Max after he'd sat down and crossed his legs over. He rested his folded hands in his lap. 'Given my current circumstances it's hard to figure out how people will react to me. You're familiar with my case I take it?'

'Oh yes' Stephanie confirmed. Max Burley had been charged with the murder of his boss Charles Maynard. 'I've seen it all in the media'.

'Well I didn't kill Charles' said Max, firmly although the tone of his voice betrayed how he was feeling inside. 'But next month I go on trial for his murder and the police believe they have a cast iron case that will see me go down for a long time. I only got bail because I've got some money in the bank that they took for security and I've never been in trouble with the police before. I have to prove my innocence before that trial starts, Miss Marshall. That's why I'm here. I need you to help me'.

'What's your lawyer doing about it?'

'Are you aware of the Sydney firm Healey and Jenkins?'

Stephanie nodded. 'Well yes I am' she confirmed. 'I've had dealings with them myself'.

'Well I'm with someone there called Brett Sandcroft' said Max. 'He's advising me to plead guilty in order to lessen my chances of a long sentence'.

'That old chestnut'.

'I know' said Max. 'If it wasn't my life we were talking about it would be laughable'.

'Can't you get some other lawyer?'

'It wouldn't make any difference because I need someone who's going to look for evidence of me being set up' said Max. 'That's what I believe has happened here, Miss Marshall. I've been set up for the murder of Charles and someone in this city is laughing over their pre dinner drink at me'.

'You have the kind of enemies who'd set you up for murder?'

'I didn't think so but someone has done a bloody good job to make it look like I killed Charles'.

'And you didn't?'

'No I didn't I had absolutely nothing to do with what happened' said Max who felt his eyes fill up. 'Absolutely nothing at all'.

'Alright, Max, don't get distressed' said Stephanie. 'You've come to the right place'.

'You mean you will help me?' he asked hopefully and leaning forward whilst wiping his cheeks free of tears. 'I'm desperate, Miss Marshall. I don't know where else to turn and you've got a reputation for getting results'

Stephanie smiled at the way he was flattering her. 'Call me Stephanie'

'Okay. Stephanie. But you can see how I'm fixed?'

'Of course I can' Stephanie went on. She could see the immense strain in those eyes. This man was clearly going through it. 'But the thing is, Max, I'll need to be sure that you are innocent and that means hearing your side of the story without it all having been filtered by journalists who are all on their own agenda. Just don't give me the same version that's appeared in the media, that's what I'm saying'.

Max sat back in his chair. 'I don't know where to start'.

'Go right back to the circumstances leading up to the death of Charles Maynard' said Stephanie. 'I know it'll be painful, Max, but please tell me everything. If there's one thing that will dissuade me from helping you it'll be if you deliberately leave anything out'.

'This isn't going to be easy'.

'No, I can imagine' said Stephanie. 'But neither is prison and if I'm going to save you from it then you're going have to convince me that I'm right in thinking you're not a killer'.

Printed in Great Britain
by Amazon.co.uk, Ltd.,
Marston Gate.